Sweet Like Sugar Cane

LEAH T. WILLIAMS

LEAH T. WILLIAMS

Author's Note

In "Neither Out Far Nor In Deep," we meet Gwendolyn Richards as a mother in America, struggling to understand her teenage son, Kadeem. But before that story, there was another - one of a young girl in St. Kitts, finding her own way through the sweet and bitter tastes of growing up.

This is that story.

- Leah T. Williams

1

"G wen, come! De funeral announcement starting and I have to do you hair before you fadda leave for factory!" Her mother's voice carried from the kitchen, mixing with the scent of fresh bread and eggs.

Gwen dragged herself from bed, instantly spotting her uniform hanging perfect and crisp by the door. Every pleat in the green skirt razor-sharp, her khaki shirt stiff with starch - her mother's handiwork from the night before. Outside, roosters were still arguing about who would announce morning first.

The kitchen radio crackled with the ominous voice reading out the day's deaths while her mother stood ready, blue jar of TCB in one hand and comb in the other. Her father sat at the small wooden table, already dressed for work at the sugar factory, sipping his tea and listening intently to hear if he knew any of the deceased.

"Sit down here," her mother commanded, pulling out a chair. "And stop making dat face before it stick so."

"It too early for all dis torture," Gwen mumbled, but sat anyway. Her mother's fingers were already working through her Jerry curl, each stroke of the comb followed by a generous dollop of activator.

"You tink is torture? Wait till you reach me age and have daughter giving you trouble every morning." Her mother's hands moved with practiced gentleness despite her complaints. "You fadda already heading to factory and you still here making style wit you face."

The mention of her father made Gwen glance his way, but he was focused on his tea, mind likely already on the machinery waiting for him at the factory. Weekends he'd be in his ground farming, but weekdays belonged to the factory's schedule.

"Lord, you hear Betty daughter gone?" Her mother paused with the comb. "Not even forty yet."

"Mmhmm," her father mumbled into his tea. "Life short for true."

By the time Sharon appeared at their gate, Gwen was fully pressed and proper, her hair gleaming, uniform immaculate.

"Morning, Miss Richards!" Sharon called out. She already had her shirt partially untucked, which made Gwen's mother suck her teeth loud enough to be heard in Sandy Point.

"Sharon, how you mudda letting you leave home wit you shirt hanging so?"

"Is fashion, Miss Richards," Sharon grinned.

"Fashion going get all you in trouble one of these days."

The morning sun was barely warming the asphalt as they walked to school, their patent leather shoes already collecting dust. The whole island was waking up - market women setting out their wares, fishing boats returning with their morning catch, uniformed students emerging from every corner.

"So," Sharon nudged Gwen's arm as they neared the school gates. "You see him yesterday?"

"Who you talking bout? Girl, you want me mudda kill me?"

"Don't play stupid. Lenwell Turnbull self. De way he watching you in assembly every morning."

"Shhhh!" Gwen looked around frantically. "You want de whole school to hear you?"

"Please, everybody already know. Even Ms. Bridgewater probably see how all you looking at each other on de landing when you tink nobody watching."

"Nobody watching nothing," Gwen protested, but her cheeks burned. Trust Sharon to notice everything - especially things that could get them both in trouble.

They joined the crowd of students gathering for morning assembly. The sea of green skirts and khaki shirts shifted in the dirt yard as everyone found their places facing the concrete stage. And there he was - Lenwell Turnbull, his almond colored skin seeming to glow in the morning sun. He moved with a confident, effortless stride, each step exuding a quiet magnetism that turned heads without the slightest hint of effort. His low-cut hair was meticulously groomed, every edge sharp and deliberate, a testament to the precision that seemed to define him—from the crispness of his clothes to the composed intensity in his gaze.

"You see?" Sharon whispered. "Even de way he walking looking like he trying to show off for somebody."

"Girl, hush you mout' before-"

A shadow fell over them. Ms. Bridgewater loomed silently, her presence more effective than any scolding. Gwen and Sharon straightened immediately, eyes forward, but Gwen could still feel Lenwell's gaze from across the yard. She didn't dare look up, but she knew if she did, she'd catch that hint of a smile he seemed to save just for her.

The headmaster's voice boomed across the yard about proper behavior and high expectations, but Gwen barely heard him. Her mind kept drifting to yesterday when she'd passed Lenwell on the landing between classes. For just a moment, their eyes had met, and something electric had passed between them. He'd opened his mouth like he wanted to speak, but then Mr. Pemberton had appeared with his geography books tucked under his arm, and the moment vanished.

Now, standing in the hot morning sun, Gwen felt that same electricity humming under her skin. First period was Geography, and Mr. Pemberton always insisted on perfect attention during his lessons about longitudes and latitudes. Last week, he'd made Marcus stand in the corner for drawing coconut trees in his notebook instead of copying the map of South America.

"Remember," Sharon whispered as they filed into class, "Mr. Pemberton say we getting test next week on dem river systems."

"Me know," Gwen replied, pulling out her notebook. Geography had always been one of her best subjects - she liked how the world made sense when laid out in neat lines and patterns on a map.

But as Mr. Pemberton began writing on the board, she felt a light touch on her shoulder. A folded piece of paper dropped onto her desk, passed forward through three pairs of hands. Her heart jumped even before she opened it.

Maybe those river systems weren't going to be as interesting as she'd thought.

2

Gwen's fingers trembled slightly as she unfolded the paper under her desk. Mr. Pemberton was busy drawing what looked like the entire Amazon River system on the board, his back turned to the class.

The note was short: "You look nice today." Just four words in neat handwriting, but they made her heart race. She knew that writing - had seen it often enough when checking her answers against his during tests.

"Gwendolyn Richards!" Mr. Pemberton's voice cracked through the air. "Since you find what's in your lap more interesting than the major tributaries of South America, perhaps you'd like to come draw them on the board?"

Heat rushed to her face as she quickly crumpled the paper in her fist. "No sir, Mr. Pemberton."

"No? Then I suggest you focus on what's in front of you rather than what's in your lap."

A few snickers rippled through the class. Gwen didn't dare turn around, but she could feel Lenwell's presence three rows back. She smoothed her notebook page and gripped her pen tightly, determined to focus on the winding blue lines Mr. Pemberton was labeling.

"Copy this down," he instructed. "It will be on your test next week."

Sharon leaned over slightly. "Wat de note say?"

"Later," Gwen whispered, not risking another scolding. But she couldn't stop her lips from curving into a small smile as she carefully traced the river routes in her notebook.

When Mr. Pemberton gathered his books and left, the class hummed with quiet conversation while they waited for the next teacher. Devon was telling some story about his weekend that had the back row trying not to laugh too loudly. Gwen caught a whiff of something that made her pause - a clean, fresh scent that reminded her of Sunday afternoons when her father would come home from working in his ground, shower, and dress for church. Those rare moments when he didn't smell like engine oil or earth, but something else entirely. She turned slightly, just enough to see Lenwell leaning forward to ask Devon something about the History homework. He glanced up, caught her looking, and that hint of a smile touched his lips again.

"You ain't fooling nobody," Sharon whispered, poking her with a pen. "De whole class could see you twisting round in you chair like you neck get spring."

"Girl, hush you mout'," Gwen hissed back, but she could feel her cheeks burning.

Mr. James strode in then, his voice already booming before he reached the desk. "Turn to page 394 - The Haitian Revolution!" He scrawled 'Toussaint L'Ouverture' across the board in his aggressive handwriting. "Today we discussing how one man changed the course of Caribbean history."

The class rustled with genuine interest. Mr. James had a way of making history feel urgent, like it was happening right outside their window instead of two hundred years ago.

"Who can tell me why L'Ouverture's leadership was different from those who came before him?"

Lenwell's hand went up, and Gwen found herself holding her breath slightly. She loved how his voice changed when he was really interested in something - deeper, more confident.

"He understood military strategy," Lenwell said, "but he also understood how to unite people. He got both free blacks and enslaved people to fight together."

"Excellent!" Mr. James launched into a passionate description of the revolution's key battles. Gwen tried to focus on taking notes, but she kept thinking about how Lenwell had sounded, how his words had carried such conviction.

The morning wore on. Ms. Netty swept in after History, her high-necked dress buttoned to her throat despite the heat. "Books away, notebooks out. We're having a pop quiz on Julius Caesar."

The class groaned in unison. Gwen opened her notebook, but her mind wasn't on Roman emperors. She was thinking about the way Lenwell spoke about revolution and justice, wondering what else he thought about when he wasn't being the quiet, proper boy everyone saw.

"Miss Richards." Ms. Netty's voice snapped her back to attention. "I trust you can tell us what Caesar's last words were?"

"Et tu, Brute," Gwen answered automatically, grateful she'd at least done the reading.

"Correct." Ms. Netty's eyes narrowed slightly, as if suspecting Gwen's mind had been elsewhere despite the right answer. "And what is the significance of these words?"

As Gwen explained about betrayal and friendship, she felt something touch her foot. A small scrap of paper had been pushed forward under the desks. With one eye on Ms. Netty, she managed to retrieve it.

"Meet me by the gate at lunch?"

Her heart jumped. She'd seen Lenwell walking to lunch before, always with the same group of boys, always turning left at the gate toward town. She'd gone the other way with Sharon, but today...

"Girl," Sharon whispered as Ms. Netty wrote on the board, "you look like you seeing jumbie. Wat dat paper say now?"

"Nothing," Gwen whispered back, but her hands were shaking slightly as she copied down the notes about Shakespeare's use of dramatic irony.

The rest of the morning crawled by. French verbs and Mathematics formulas blurred together as Gwen watched the sun climb higher outside the classroom windows. When the lunch bell finally rang, Sharon was already standing, coins jingling in her skirt pocket.

"You coming?"

Gwen hesitated, smoothing her skirt. "I... might go different way today."

Sharon's eyes narrowed, then widened with understanding. "Girl! You mean to tell me-"

"Shhhh!"

"Well," Sharon grinned, "make sure you tell me everything after."

Gwen gathered her things slowly, heart pounding. Through the window, she could see students streaming out the gate, breaking into their usual lunch groups. Then she saw him, standing slightly apart from the others, waiting.

She took a deep breath and stood. Whatever happened next would change everything.

3

Gwen paused at the gate, her hand smoothing her skirt for the hundredth time. Groups of students were already heading in different directions toward the various houses that sold lunch.

"We could walk together?" His voice was closer than she expected, making her jump slightly. That clean Sunday scent wrapped around her as he fell into step beside her. "If you want."

She managed to nod, suddenly unsure what to do with her hands. The coins in her pocket felt heavy, reminding her she needed to actually buy lunch, not just float along in this dream-like state where Lenwell Turnbull was walking next to her.

"You usually go by de pink house?" he asked.

"Yeah."

"Me too." That smile again, the one that made her stomach flutter. "Devon and them like going other places, but de food at de pink house better."

They walked in silence for a moment, both hyperaware of the space between them, of other students passing by. A group of fourth form girls whispered and giggled as they passed. Gwen focused on her shoes against the dusty road.

"I liked what you said," she found herself saying. "In History. About L'Ouverture."

"Yeah?" He looked pleased. "Most people think History boring, but Mr. James does make it feel real, you know?"

"Like how?"

"Like..." he paused, considering. "Like how things people do could change everything around them. How one person standing up could make others stand up too."

She liked how his voice got deeper when he talked about things that interested him, how his hands moved as he explained.

"You always so quiet in class," he said. "But I see you writing everything down."

"Just because somebody quiet don't mean they no got nothing to say."

His smile widened. "So what you got to say then?"

She felt bold suddenly. "Maybe you have to wait and find out."

The scent of cooking food grew stronger as they approached the pink house - curry, rice, stew chicken, and the unmistakable aroma of fresh beef patties. Other students were already clustering around the door.

"You ever try de spicy patty?" Lenwell asked as they joined the line.

"Try it? Boy, me does eat two, three at once sometimes."

He raised his eyebrows. "For true? Most people can't handle de heat."

"Most people weak," she grinned. "Me mudda does make pepper sauce that could burn de paint off a car."

When they reached the front of the line, Lenwell ordered first. "Two spicy patty, please."

"Make that four," Gwen added, pulling her coins from her pocket. "Me no come all this way for just one patty."

The woman behind the counter smiled as she wrapped their orders, the paper already showing spots of grease. The patties were still hot enough to burn fingers.

They found a spot in the shade of a nearby tree to eat. Gwen bit into her first patty without hesitation, the spice hitting immediately. Lenwell watched, impressed, as she didn't even reach for water.

"You no playing bout handling heat," he said, taking a bite of his own.

"Me tell you already. But everybody think because somebody quiet, they weak too."

"Nobody who know you going think you weak after seeing you eat these patties like they sweet bread."

She laughed. "You should see me wit pepper sauce. Me fadda does say me born wit steel tongue."

They ate in comfortable silence for a moment, the sounds of other students' conversations drifting around them. The patties were perfect - flaky crust, spicy beef filling, just the right amount of heat to make your eyes water but not enough to overwhelm the flavor.

"You want to walk back together?" Lenwell asked as they finished eating.

Gwen brushed pastry crumbs from her skirt. "Well, yeah. Me no come here by meself, you know."

His laugh was unexpected and genuine. "True true. Me just making sure you no planning to disappear on me."

"Disappear where? School still going on whole afternoon."

"Good point." He stood, offering his hand to help her up. After a slight hesitation, she took it, trying to ignore the flutter in her stomach at the contact.

They walked back toward school, talking about nothing and everything - about how Mr. Pemberton's voice got higher when he was excited about rivers, about the way Ms. Netty's dress always looked like it was choking her, about Sharon's uncanny ability to fall asleep sitting straight up in French class.

"She does drool sometimes too," Gwen confided, making Lenwell laugh again.

"You mean to tell me all this time me thinking Sharon paying attention, she really sleeping?"

"Girl could sleep through hurricane if you let her. One time she sleep straight through de headmaster assembly. Only wake up when everybody singing de national anthem."

At the gate, Lenwell paused. "Maybe we could do this again tomorrow?"

"Maybe," she said, but they both knew she meant yes.

As they headed back to class, Gwen could feel other students watching, could hear the whispers starting. But somehow, with the taste of spicy patties still on her tongue and the memory of Lenwell's laugh in her ears, she found she didn't mind at all.

4

Saturday mornings always started before the sun. Gwen's father would knock once on her door - just once - and she knew better than to make him wait. Through her window, she could see his old blue VW Bug parked in its usual spot while the truck they used only for ground sat ready for the mountain trip.

"Gwen!" Her mother's voice carried from the kitchen. "Make sure you take something to tie up you hair. Last time you come back looking like you been fighting wit de bushes and de bushes win."

The kitchen smelled of fresh mint tea, the leaves picked from right outside their backdoor where her mother grew all kinds of bush for tea. Her mother stood at the counter wrapping food - salt fish and johnny cakes for their breakfast up in the mountains. Dark circles shadowed her eyes lately, but her hands moved quick and sure as she packed their provisions.

"You feeling okay, mammy?" Gwen asked. Her mother had been going to bed earlier these past weeks, something about tiredness she couldn't shake.

"Chile, everybody feel tired sometimes. Life hard but me harder." She handed Gwen the wrapped package. "Make sure you fadda eat something before he start working. Man does think he running on air and sunshine alone."

Steam rose from the mint tea her mother poured into an old flask for them to take up the mountain. Outside, the sky was just beginning to lighten. Her father waited in the truck, which groaned up steep roads that seemed to get narrower the higher they climbed. Others were already heading to their grounds too - men and women with tools over their shoulders, children trailing behind carrying water bottles and food wraps.

"Morning, Mr. Richards!" A woman called out as they passed. "Ground looking good these days!"

"Morning, Miss Mary," her father called back. "Your peas coming in good too."

"Got to feed these children somehow," Miss Mary laughed. "Shop price too high these days."

Gwen noticed her father nodding. He didn't say much, but she knew he thought the same way - better to grow your own food than depend on buying everything. The factory work paid the bills, but the ground fed them.

They parked where the road ended and the real climbing began. Their plot sat higher than most, which meant hauling water up but also meant better drainage when the rains came. Her father handed her a hoe and took up his machete.

"Watch where you stepping," he reminded her as they climbed. "Centipede no send letter to tell you he coming."

The sun was properly rising now, painting the eastern sky in shades of pink and gold. Below them, Lodge sprawled out toward the sea, houses looking like tiny boxes from this height. Somewhere down there, her mother would be starting her real Saturday routine - cleaning, cooking, maybe resting if the tiredness got too heavy.

And somewhere down there, Lenwell was probably just waking up. The thought made her cheeks warm, remembering their lunch together yesterday. Sharon had practically exploded with questions afterward.

"Girl, you head in de clouds or you going help me clear these weeds?" Her father's voice broke through her thoughts.

"Sorry, daddy." She gripped the hoe tighter and got to work. The rhythm of it was familiar - check the ground first, then dig careful around the young plants, pile the weeds to use for mulch later. Everything in the ground had its purpose, even the things you pulled up.

They worked steadily as the sun climbed higher. Her father moved ahead, clearing the tall grass around the edges of their plot. Sometimes he'd pause to point something out - which plants needed more water, which ones were ready for harvesting, which ones were showing signs of trouble.

"See how dat one turning yellow?" He indicated a young tomato plant. "Dat mean he hungry. Ground too tired there, need feeding."

"How you know all this stuff, daddy?" She watched him crumble something into the soil around the plant's base.

"Same way you know all dem book learning - some-body teach me, and then I learn more by doing." He straightened up, stretching his back. "But book learning and ground learning, they both important. You just got to know which one to use when."

They broke for breakfast around nine, settling on a relatively flat spot with a view of the valley. The salt fish and johnny cakes had grown cold, but hunger made them taste perfect anyway. A breeze carried the scent of someone's cook fire - probably Miss Mary or one of the others burning dried bush they'd cleared.

"You been quiet lately," her father said, carefully wrapping the remaining food back up. "Everything alright at school?"

Gwen's heart jumped, thinking of Lenwell. But her father wasn't looking at her - he was gazing out over Lodge, his expression thoughtful.

"School good," she said carefully. "Mr. Pemberton say I doing good in Geography."

"Mmhmm." He took a long drink of the mint tea. "You mudda say she notice you taking more care wit you appearance these days."

Heat crept up Gwen's neck. Trust her mother to notice everything. "Just trying to look neat, dat's all."

Her father was quiet for a moment. Then: "You know why I still working this ground even though I got factory job?"

The sudden change of subject caught her off guard. "Because shop price too high?"

He smiled slightly. "Dat too. But more than dat. Ground does teach you things factory can't. Like how everything got its season. You can't rush corn to grow faster by pulling on it. You can't make rain fall by wishing. Some things just take the time they take."

Gwen had a feeling he wasn't just talking about farming anymore, but before she could respond, a distant roll of thunder made them both look up. Dark clouds were gathering over the mountain's peak.

"Rain coming," her father said, standing. "We better finish what we can before it reach."

They worked faster then, racing the approaching storm. Other farmers were packing up too, calling out warnings to each other about the weather. Just as the first heavy drops began to fall, her father declared they'd done enough for one Saturday.

The drive down was slower than the drive up - the rain made the narrow roads slick, and her father took no chances with his old truck on these curves. They passed Miss Mary hurrying home under a large piece of plastic, her children squealing as the rain found its way under their makeshift shelter.

"You want to stop and give them a ride?" Gwen asked.

Her father was already slowing down. "Go make space in the back."

By the time they reached home, the rain was falling in earnest. They were all soaked despite their best efforts - Miss Mary and her children, Gwen and her father, even the vegetables they'd harvested. But everyone was laughing.

"Lord!" Her mother exclaimed when they trooped in. "All you look like you been swimming with clothes on!"

"Rain catch us," Miss Mary explained, "but you husband kind enough to save us from drowning on de road."

"Well, come in properly and let me fix all you some fresh bush tea before you catch you death."

Gwen helped her mother with the tea while her father and Miss Mary discussed the weather's effect on their crops. The children perched on kitchen chairs, swinging their legs and eyeing the bag of cheese curls on top of the refrigerator.

Looking at them all - wet but warm, laughing and talking in their steamy kitchen - Gwen felt something settle in her chest. This was what her father meant about things having their season, about not rushing what needed time to grow. Some things, like vegetables and wisdom and maybe even love, just needed the right conditions to flourish.

She thought about Lenwell, about their careful conversations just beginning to bloom. Maybe that too would grow in its own time, like her father's tomatoes - with proper care and patience and just the right amount of nurturing.

Her mother caught her daydreaming and raised an eyebrow, but said nothing. Instead, she just smiled and pushed the cheese curls toward Miss Mary's children.

Outside, the rain continued to fall, washing the mountain's red dirt from their tools, feeding the grounds they'd just left, promising new growth for tomorrow.

5

When Geography finished, Sharon stretched dramatically in her seat. "Me hand about to fall off from all dat writing bout rivers."

"At least you was writing," Gwen said. "Half de class look like they fall asleep when Mr. Pemberton voice start getting high like when baby goat crying for he mudda."

"You mean like how you been writing, or just staring at you paper and smiling?"

"Girl, hush you mout'." But Gwen couldn't help smiling again as Lenwell turned around in his seat.

"All you going for lunch?"

The walk to the pink house was different now that Lenwell joined them. Sharon kept the conversation flowing, but Gwen found herself aware of every time their hands accidentally brushed as they walked, of how he moved slightly closer when other students pushed past them on the narrow path.

The pink house was busy as usual, the scent of curry and fresh beef patties making Gwen's stomach growl. While they waited in line, Sharon told them about her little brother's latest disaster with their mother's good sheets and a mango stain that wouldn't come out.

"He try tell we mudda dat de mango jump out he hand by itself," Sharon said, rolling her eyes. "Like mango got wings now."

When they reached the counter, Lenwell stepped back slightly. "You go first."

"Ever de gentleman," Sharon teased, but Gwen noticed how his fingers brushed against hers as she moved past him, so quickly she might have imagined it.

They found a spot in the shade to eat, Sharon keeping them laughing with her impression of Ms. Netty's face when someone had suggested they study Romeo and Juliet instead of Julius Caesar.

"She look like somebody put pepper sauce in she tea," Sharon said, making that same pinched expression.

Even Lenwell, usually so controlled, couldn't help laughing. The sound made Gwen glance up, catching his eyes on her. He looked away quickly, but something warm bloomed in her chest.

The walk back to school dragged, their footsteps heavy with reluctance, the afternoon sun pressing down like a weighted hand. The air shimmered with heat, making the prospect of returning to class even less appealing. Other students wove past them, laughter and shouted greetings punctuating the thick, drowsy air.

A sudden rush of bodies jostled them, and for the briefest moment, Gwen was pressed against Lenwell's side. His hand found her elbow—steady, warm, fleeting. The contact lasted only a second, but the ghost of his touch lingered, a soft, electrifying imprint on her skin long after they pulled apart.

In her kitchen that evening, Gwen watched her mother cooking. The familiar movements were slower now, each task taking just a little more effort than it used to.

"Mammy, you want me get dat pot for you?"

"No chile. Last time you try help in here we almost have to call fire brigade." Her mother paused to rest against the counter. "Just sit there where I could see you and tell me bout you day."

So Gwen talked about Mr. Pemberton's rivers and Sharon's stories, carefully not mentioning how her skin still tingled where Lenwell's fingers had touched her arm, or how his laugh made her stomach flip in ways that had nothing to do with hunger.

Her mother stirred the pot slowly, adding seasonings without measuring. "Sharon still eating lunch wit you?"

"Yeah. She still de same Sharon - always got story to tell."

Her mother nodded but said nothing else, just continued stirring. The kitchen filled with the scent of garlic and thyme, familiar spices that meant home and safety and the things that didn't need to be said out loud.

After dinner, Gwen sat at her desk trying to focus on Geography homework. But her mind kept drifting to those small moments - a brushed hand, a caught glance, a gentle touch - each one tiny but significant, like the first drops of rain before a storm.

6

Gwen hung her uniform on the back of her bedroom door, far from the kitchen's cooking smells. Her mother had pressed it the night before in the front room, each pleat sharp enough to cut paper. These days, Gwen found herself taking extra care - keeping her uniforms away from the kitchen, hanging them where no food scents could cling to the fabric.

"Gwen?" Her mother's voice carried from the kitchen. "You going stand there all morning admiring you uniform or you coming to get some breakfast?"

"Coming, mammy." But first she carefully draped a clean sheet over the uniform to protect it.

Her mother's eyebrows rose when Gwen finally appeared in the kitchen. "Since when you so particular bout you clothes? Time was you would iron you uniform right here next to de stove."

"Just trying to look neat," Gwen mumbled, sliding into her usual chair but keeping well back from the pot of garlic-scented stew her mother stirred.

"Neat enough to wrap up you uniform like it going in museum?" Her mother's eyes held that knowing look. "Well, at least you in here now. Keep me company while me cook."

"Just watching though," Gwen clarified quickly. "Me know better than to touch anything."

"Good. Because me still ain't recover from de fish incident."

"Mammy! How me supposed to know you can't fry fish without oil?"

"Chile, is common sense! Even de sound tell you something wrong when de fish hitting de dry pan like somebody beating drum."

At school, Sharon eyed Gwen's pristine uniform. "Well look at you, Gwen! Like you going meet de Queen or something."

"Girl, hush you mout'. Me just want look neat."

"Neat? You collar so stiff it could stand up by itself!"

Before Gwen could respond, Lenwell walked in. His uniform was immaculate as always, each pleat perfect, his shoes shining. Their eyes met briefly before both looked away.

"Lord," Sharon muttered. "All we wearing de same thing and still all you finding way to notice each other special."

Geography passed in a blur of river systems and ocean currents. Mr. Pemberton's voice rose with excitement as he described water patterns, but Gwen's mind wandered far from maps and tributaries, her hand copying notes automatically while her thoughts drifted.

A folded paper appeared on her desk. "You uniform looking nice today," it read in Lenwell's neat handwriting. "Like how de sun catch de pleats."

Sharon, reading over her shoulder, rolled her eyes. "He do know everybody wearing de same thing, right? Same green skirt, same khaki shirt, same everything."

"But some people wear it different," Lenwell said softly from behind them. Something in his quiet confidence made Gwen's cheeks warm.

At lunch, Sharon created their moment without being obvious about it. "Jennifer!" she called suddenly. "Wait up! Me want ask you bout dat thing!" And she was gone, leaving them alone in line.

"Sharon right though," Lenwell said as they waited. "We all wearing de same thing."

"Yeah."

"But nobody wear it quite like you." His voice was soft, meant just for her.

Their hands brushed as they moved forward in line, and this time neither pulled away immediately. Just that small touch felt significant, like something shifting beneath still water.

That evening, Gwen hovered in the kitchen doorway while her mother cooked.

"You can come in, you know," her mother said, stirring the pot. "De food not going jump out and attack you uniform."

"Me know. Just... comfortable here."

Her mother shook her head but smiled. "Tell me bout you day then, from way over there."

"Nothing much happen," Gwen said, but she couldn't keep from smiling.

"Nothing much got Gwen smiling like that? Must be some special kind of nothing."

Before Gwen could protest, her father's heavy steps sounded on the back stairs. He entered still in his factory clothes, bringing the scent of machinery with him.

"What all this talk bout school?" he asked, heading for the sink to wash his hands.

"Nothing," they said together, which made them share a secret smile.

Her father looked between them, shaking his head slightly. "Long as nobody burning down we kitchen."

"Me not even allowed to touch nothing in here anyway," Gwen said, that familiar heat rising in her voice. "Every time anybody mention cooking, all you have to bring up every little thing-"

"Little thing?" her mother interrupted, but she was fighting a smile. "You call nearly burning down we house little thing?"

Gwen opened her mouth to argue, but caught her father's steady look - that calm gaze that could settle storms - and felt the fight drain out of her.

Later in her room, she checked her uniform for the next day, making sure it still hung well away from any cooking smells. Same green skirt, same khaki shirt as everyone else. But maybe Sharon was right - maybe it wasn't what you wore but how you wore it that mattered.

She smiled, remembering Lenwell's note, the way his eyes had found hers across the classroom. Same uniform as everyone else, but somehow, when he looked at her, she felt anything but ordinary.

7

Save by the Bell flickered on the TV screen while Gwen finished her homework on the living room floor. Lisa strutted down the hallway in another perfect outfit she'd probably designed herself, tossing out quick comebacks that made everyone laugh. That's what Gwen loved about Lisa - she had style, but she also had spirit.

"You watching that American nonsense again?" her mother asked, pausing in her ironing.

"Is not nonsense, mammy. Lisa smart - she make all she own clothes and everything."

"Smart?" Her mother laughed. "Since when American school look anything like here? Them children walking round in all kind of fancy clothes, coming and going as they please."

"Well, Lisa would probably design something nice, even with we uniform."

Her mother just shook her head, but she was smiling. "Do you homework properly instead of dreaming bout American fashion."

The next afternoon, the sun hung heavy as they left school, turning everything golden-hazy. Sharon walked between Gwen and Lenwell as usual, telling them about her little brother's latest drama.

"He tell we mudda de dog eat he homework. We ain't even got dog!" Sharon's hands flew as she talked. "But you know what de worst part is?"

"What?" Gwen asked, but she was distracted by how the sun caught Lenwell's profile when he laughed at Sharon's story.

"De worst part is she believe him! Say maybe was de neighbor dog come through we fence. Like homework so sweet that dog want eat it."

They passed the usual groups heading home - younger students running and shoving, older ones walking slower, everyone's uniform wilting in the heat. The road stretched ahead, lined on both sides with tall sugar cane, the stalks swaying gently in the afternoon breeze.

"Oh!" Sharon stopped suddenly. "Me forget me supposed to go by Jennifer house. She fadda bring back some stuff from town for we mudda."

"You want us wait?" Gwen asked, but Sharon was already backing away with a too-innocent smile.

"Nah, all you go ahead. Me know where to find you tomorrow."

Then it was just the two of them, walking beside the towering cane fields. The sudden quiet made Gwen's heart beat faster, each step feeling significant somehow.

"Sharon and she stories," Lenwell said finally, his voice soft in the afternoon hush.

"Yeah. She something else."

They walked a few more steps in silence. The breeze moved through the cane, making the stalks whisper against each other. Gwen found herself noticing everything with sharp clarity - how their shadows stretched long beside them on the dusty road, how the heat made everything feel slower and dreamlike, how Lenwell's hand brushed against hers with each step.

When their fingers finally linked together, it felt both surprising and inevitable. His palm was warm against hers, slightly rough from football, but gentle too. They walked like that for a while, not speaking, just holding hands in the golden light while birds called overhead and the sugar cane swayed around them.

At a bend in the road, where the cane grew particularly tall and thick, Lenwell stopped. When Gwen turned to ask why, the words died in her throat. The way he was looking at her made everything else fade away - the heat, the dust, the calling birds.

He reached up slowly, giving her time to move away if she wanted, and touched her cheek. His fingers were soft against her skin, trembling slightly. Or maybe she was the one trembling. Maybe they both were.

The first brush of his lips against hers was gentle, hesitant. A question more than a kiss. Gwen answered by pressing closer, her free hand gripping his shirt sleeve while their linked hands tightened together.

Time seemed to stop, or maybe stretch out like warm toffee. Everything narrowed to this moment - the softness of his mouth, the sugar cane whispering around them, the late afternoon sun painting everything in shades of gold.

When they finally pulled apart, neither moved far. Lenwell rested his forehead against hers, both of them breathing a little faster than normal.

"Me been wanting to do that for long time," he whispered.

"Yeah?"

"Yeah." His thumb brushed over her knuckles where their hands were still joined. "Just had to find de right moment."

A breeze stirred the cane, making the leaves rustle like applause. Gwen felt herself smiling, unable to stop even if she'd wanted to. When Lenwell smiled back, that special smile that seemed meant just for her, she thought her heart might burst from happiness.

They walked the rest of the way home holding hands, talking about nothing and everything, stealing glances at each other and breaking into grins each time their eyes met. At her gate, he squeezed her hand once before letting go.

"Tomorrow?" he asked.

"Tomorrow," she agreed.

Inside, her mother took one look at her face and raised an eyebrow, but said nothing. Some things, Gwen was learning, didn't need to be said out loud to be understood perfectly well.

Later, doing homework at her desk, she caught herself touching her lips, remembering. The sugar cane leaves had whispered around them like secrets, the afternoon sun had turned everything golden, and his hand in hers had felt like the beginning of something real. Something that was perfectly, completely their own.

8

"You never even tell me nothing!" Sharon cornered Gwen before first class. "Me have to find out from Jennifer who hear from she cousin who see all you behind de cane field!"

"Shhhh!" Gwen looked around frantically, but the landing was noisy with students settling in for the day. "Nothing happen."

"Nothing? Then how come Jennifer cousin say she see all you holding hands looking like you forget anybody else exist in de world?"

Heat crept up Gwen's neck. "Since when Jennifer cousin watching we business anyway?"

"Chile, everybody business is everybody business round here. You know that." Sharon's stern expression broke into a grin. "So? How it was?"

Before Gwen could answer, Ms. Bridgewater appeared at the door, her presence silencing the room more effectively than any shout could have. Gwen slid into her seat, aware of Lenwell behind her, remembering how his hand had felt against her cheek.

"The properties of triangles," Ms. Bridgewater began writing on the board, but Gwen's mind kept drifting to other properties - like how the afternoon sun had painted everything gold, how sugar cane leaves could hide two people from the world.

A light touch on her shoulder made her jump. Lenwell was passing papers back, his fingers lingering just a moment longer than necessary. Such a small thing, but it sent warmth spreading through her chest.

"Miss Richards," Ms. Bridgewater's voice cut through her daydream. "Perhaps you'd like to explain the difference between isosceles and equilateral triangles?"

Gwen straightened in her seat, forced her mind back to geometry. "Yes, Miss. An isosceles triangle has two equal sides, but an equilateral has all three sides equal."

The teacher's eyes narrowed slightly, like she'd been expecting Gwen to stumble. "Correct. Though you might pay more attention to the board than to whatever's so interesting behind you."

A few students snickered. Gwen felt her face burn, but then a small folded paper appeared on her desk.

"You getting we in trouble already," it read in Lenwell's neat writing. When she glanced back, he was focused on his notebook, but his lips twitched with a suppressed smile.

At lunch, Sharon created their moment without being obvious about it. "Jennifer!" she called as they neared the pink house. "Wait fa me! You never tell me what you cousin say bout-"

"Sharon!" Gwen tried to grab her friend's arm, but Sharon was already gone, laughing as she joined Jennifer.

"She not very subtle," Lenwell said softly beside her.

"No," Gwen agreed. "But she me good friend still."

They got their food and found a spot in the shade. Without Sharon's constant chatter, the silence felt different - charged with something new and delicate.

"You get in trouble in Math?" he asked finally.

"Nah. Ms. Bridgewater always looking for something to say."

"True. But maybe me was distracting you little bit."

She looked up to find him watching her, that same gentle intensity from yesterday making her heart skip. "Maybe little bit," she admitted.

His smile then was like sunshine breaking through clouds. Under the cover of their lunch wrappings, his fingers found hers, and they sat like that while they ate - holding hands and stealing glances and trying not to grin too obviously.

The walk home felt different too. Sharon still walked with them, but now she drifted ahead sometimes, giving them space without making it obvious. When their hands brushed, neither pulled away.

"Me getting better at this," Gwen said as they passed the cane fields.

"At what?"

"Walking and holding you hand at de same time without tripping over me own feet."

His laugh was soft. "Good thing you learning quick then. Would hate to have to catch you every time."

"You would catch me though?"

He squeezed her hand. "Every time."

Behind them, Sharon made a gagging noise. "Lord, all you sweet like sugar. Me going get cavity just from walking with you two."

But Gwen saw her friend's pleased smile, the way she looked between them like she was proud of her matchmaking.

At her gate, Lenwell let go of her hand reluctantly. In broad daylight, with neighbors potentially watching, they couldn't do more than share a look. But that look held yesterday's kiss and tomorrow's promise.

"Tomorrow?" he asked, just like yesterday.

"Tomorrow," she agreed.

Inside, she found her mother in the kitchen, humming as she stirred a pot. The familiar scent of garlic and thyme filled the air, but her mother's movements seemed slower than usual, like each stir took more effort.

"You looking happy these days," her mother said, not turning around.

"Just having good day, mammy."

Her mother hummed knowingly but said nothing else. The pot bubbled, the spoon scraped rhythmically, and outside birds called as the sun began its slow descent.

Everything was the same as always, but somehow completely different.

9

Gwen found herself studying Lenwell more openly now - the way the sun brought out honey-colored flecks in his warm, sunk-kissed complexion with golden undertones, how his short neat haircut emphasized his strong jawline, the grace in his long fingers when he wrote notes. Sometimes he'd catch her looking and smile that slow smile that made her stomach flip.

"You staring again," Sharon whispered during History.

"No me ain't."

"Yes you is. Like how he does stare at you too when you writing, like he counting you eyelashes or something."

The talk had started, as it always did in a place where everybody knew everybody. Whispers about how often they were seen walking together, how they always seemed to find reasons to be near each other in class.

"You dey wit each other now?" Jennifer asked at lunch, sliding onto the bench next to Sharon.

"Why everybody so interested in we business?" Gwen asked, but she felt Lenwell's hand brush against hers under the table.

"Come nuh," Sharon cut in, grabbing Jennifer's arm. "Me want show you something."

As Sharon dragged Jennifer away, Gwen caught the knowing look between her friend and Lenwell. Their silent agreement to protect this new thing growing between them made her chest warm.

That afternoon, instead of heading straight home, Lenwell tugged gently on her hand. "Come. Me want show you something."

He led her down a path she'd passed many times but never taken, winding between thick bushes until suddenly the sea spread out before them. This stretch of beach was hidden from the main road, protected by natural rock formations that curved like arms around a small cove.

"How you find this place?"

"Been coming here since me small," he said. "When me want peace and quiet."

The late sun painted everything gold - the sand, the water, the smooth rocks. Something about the privacy of it, the way the rest of the world seemed far away, made Gwen's heart beat faster.

"Water looking nice," Lenwell said softly.

Gwen watched the waves catch the light. "Too nice to just watch."

They looked at each other for a long moment. Then Lenwell grinned. "We could..."

"In we uniform?"

"Under." His voice was quiet, uncertain. "If you want."

Heat crept up her neck, but not from embarrassment. This felt right somehow - like everything between them, both scary and natural at the same time.

"Turn round," Gwen said softly. They stood back to back, the sound of fabric rustling mixing with the waves. Gwen's fingers trembled as she unbuttoned her shirt, slipped off her skirt. The air felt electric on her skin.

"You done?" Lenwell asked, his voice catching slightly.

"Yeah."

They turned slowly. Gwen felt exposed in her blue cotton underwear, but the way Lenwell looked at her - like she was something precious and beautiful - made her feel brave instead of shy. Her eyes traced the lean muscles of his chest, the smooth brown skin she'd only imagined before.

When their eyes met, something shifted in the air between them. Without speaking, they moved toward the water together.

The sea was warm, perfect. Lenwell's height advantage disappeared as they floated, their heads close together while their feet kicked lazily to stay up. Drops of water clung to his eyelashes, making them sparkle in the golden light.

"You look different like this," he said, watching how her glossy, springy curls formed swirling patterns on the water.

"Good different or bad different?"

"Just different." He moved closer, one hand finding her waist under the water. "Like how everything different with you, but in de best way."

When he kissed her this time, it was unlike their hidden kisses in the cane fields. Salt water and sunshine mixed on their lips. The waves rocked them gently together, making everything dreamlike. Gwen's arms wound around his neck while his hands steadied her waist, keeping them afloat. She could feel his heart beating fast against hers, or maybe that was her own heart. Maybe they were beating the same rhythm now.

They broke apart only when a larger wave threatened to submerge them. Lenwell's eyes were dark and intense when they met hers, full of things neither of them were ready to say out loud.

Later, they sat on the sand letting the breeze dry them before putting their uniforms back on. The setting sun turned everything to fire - the water, the sand, the droplets in Lenwell's eyelashes.

"We should go soon," Gwen said reluctantly. "Before it get dark."

"Yeah." But neither moved. These moments felt precious somehow, like holding water in cupped hands.

At home that evening, she found her mother in the kitchen, sitting more often now between stirring the pot.

"You looking happy," her mother observed. "Something good happen at school?"

Gwen talked about safe things instead - about how Sharon's little brother had finally admitted no dog ate his homework, about the new girl in class who'd moved from

Nevis and was still mixing up teachers' names, about the excitement over the upcoming sports day.

Her mother listened, stirring slowly. "You walking like you floating these days."

"Me just happy, mammy."

"Mmhmm." Her mother's knowing look spoke volumes. "Just remember - clouds nice to look at, but they ain't solid ground for standing on."

Later, doing homework at her desk, Gwen's uniform still smelled faintly of sea salt. Through her window, she could see the moon rising over the cane fields, turning everything silver instead of the gold she was used to from afternoon walks. Different light, different perspective, but the same sweet feeling in her chest when she thought about how Lenwell had looked at her in the water, like she was something rare and precious.

She touched her lips, remembering their salt-water kisses. Let people talk. Some things were worth whatever storms might come, solid ground or not.

10

"But Miss," Sharon's voice cut through the quiet classroom. "If Shakespeare dead so long, why we still have to learn bout he?"

Ms. Netty's spine stiffened. The entire class held its breath - everyone knew that tone in Sharon's voice, the one that usually ended with trouble.

"Because, Miss James, some things transcend death." Ms. Netty's words came out clipped and precise. "Though if you continue questioning my curriculum choices, you might find out exactly how temporary life can be."

"Me just saying," Sharon continued, either not seeing or ignoring Gwen's warning look. "We got plenty good stories right here that we could-"

"Miss James." Ms. Netty's voice could have frozen the Caribbean Sea. "Come to the front."

The silence in the classroom grew heavier. Sharon stood slowly, her chair scraping against the floor. Gwen's hands gripped her desk edge as her friend walked to the front, that stubborn set to her shoulders that meant she wasn't sorry at all.

"Hold out your arm."

The leather belt appeared from Ms. Netty's desk drawer. Six sharp cracks split the air, leaving angry red marks on Sharon's brown skin. She didn't cry out, but Gwen saw her friend's jaw clench with each strike.

"Now," Ms. Netty said, returning the belt to her drawer, "shall we continue with Macbeth?"

Sharon returned to her seat, eyes bright with unshed tears but chin still high. Under her desk, Gwen squeezed her friend's hand. She felt Lenwell shift in his seat behind them, knew he was remembering all the times Sharon had covered for them, created moments for them.

The rest of the class passed in tense silence. When the bell rang, Sharon was first out the door. Gwen started to follow, but Lenwell caught her hand.

"Let her cool off a little bit," he said softly. "She gan need space."

They took the long way home, through the cane fields where the afternoon sun turned everything golden. Without Sharon's chatter, they walked in comfortable silence until Gwen spotted a particularly good stalk.

Her hands moved with practiced confidence, twisting the cane just so. The clean snap was satisfying, like proving something to herself.

"You good at that," Lenwell said, watching her strip the outer layer with quick, sure movements.

"Been doing it since before me could walk proper." She held a piece to his lips, something electric passing between them when he took it, his mouth brushing her fingers.

"Sweet," he said softly.

They shared pieces as they walked, taking turns feeding each other, making the ordinary act of eating sugar cane feel like something special, something secret. The world around them faded—the rustling trees, the distant chatter of other students—until only the quiet rhythm of their footsteps and the lingering taste of sugar remained.

But all moments, no matter how sweet, had to end.

By the time she reached home, the warmth of the afternoon had settled into the house, the scent of simmering food wrapping around her like a familiar embrace. Her mother sat in her usual kitchen chair, the pot bubbling on the stove.

"Mammy? You alright?"

"Just resting me eyes a little bit." Her mother straightened with visible effort. "Come stir this before it stick."

Gwen approached the pot cautiously - her cooking disasters were legendary in the family. But stirring she could manage, especially with her mother's watchful eye.

"You hands looking sticky," her mother observed with a small smile. "Sugar cane?"

"Maybe little bit."

They worked in comfortable silence, Gwen stirring while her mother cut seasonings with increasingly slow movements. Through the kitchen window, the sun painted the sky in shades of pink and gold, another day ending in their own familiar rhythm.

11

The classroom felt empty without Sharon. Her desk stood silent while they waited for the teacher to arrive. That empty space seemed to mock them, especially when their teacher swept in, her eyes lingering on Sharon's spot with something like satisfaction.

"Where she be?" Lenwell whispered from behind Gwen.

"She say she staying home," Gwen whispered back. "She hands still burning from yesterday."

But they both knew it wasn't her hands that hurt most. Sharon's pride was a different kind of wound.

A folded paper appeared on Gwen's desk during class. "Meet me by de old house?" Just a few words, but they made her pulse quicken. She knew where he meant - everybody knew about the old wooden house where people went to smoke or skip class. She'd walked past it hundred times, pretending not to see the older students slipping away there, but she'd never gone herself.

Until today.

When afternoon classes started, she raised her hand. "Please sir, me need the bathroom."

Her heart thundered as she walked down the corridor, past the regular bathrooms, toward the back stairs. She hesitated at the top step. Good girls didn't skip class. Good girls didn't meet boys in secret.

But Lenwell was waiting at the bottom of the stairs, and something in his eyes made her feet move forward.

"You sure?" he asked softly.

She wasn't, but she nodded anyway.

They walked quickly, not touching, not speaking. The wooden house appeared through the trees, small and weathered but still standing. Its verandah wrapped around two sides, creating hidden corners away from passing eyes. The wood creaked under their feet as they found a spot behind an old column.

"Everybody come here," Lenwell said, his voice low. "But never feel right before."

"Why now?" Her own voice sounded strange to her ears.

Instead of answering, he kissed her. Not like their careful kisses in the cane fields - this was different, hungry. His hands found her waist, pulling her closer. She could feel his heart racing against hers as her fingers tangled in his shirt.

"Gwen..." His breath was warm against her neck.

Something shifted between them then. His hands grew bolder, exploring her back, her sides. Her own courage surprised her as she pressed closer, letting him pull her against him until there was no space left.

They learned each other in fragments - the soft spot behind his ear that made him gasp, how his fingers on her bare waist made her shiver. Time seemed to stop existing, measured only in heartbeats and touches.

A bell rang in the distance, shocking them apart. Reality crashed back - they'd missed half of class, their uniforms were crushed, Gwen's curls were losing their definition, soft tendrils breaking free in little spirals.

"We got to go," she whispered, though her body protested the idea of moving.

They straightened uniforms with shaking hands, trying to erase the evidence of their afternoon. The walk back was faster, urgent with the fear of being caught.

At home that evening, her mother was moving slower between the pots, each motion careful and measured.

"You looking flushed," her mother said. "Everything alright?"

"Just the heat, mammy."

But her mother's eyes held something knowing. "You father working late at de factory. Say Saturday he going market early - want you come help him sell he ground provisions."

Gwen nodded, grateful for the change of subject. Through the kitchen window, the sun was setting behind the cane fields. Somewhere out there was a wooden house holding new secrets, new understanding of how life could rush forward when you weren't looking, carrying you along like a river after rain.

12

Dawn was just a promise in the sky when Gwen's father knocked on her door. By the time she reached the kitchen, he had already loaded the truck with provisions from their ground.

Her mother pressed a wrapped package into her hands. "Make sure you eat before the heat catch you."

The old truck groaned as they started down the road, the eastern sky turning pink behind them. They passed through Lodge, houses still dark except for the odd kitchen light where somebody else was preparing for market day.

"De mango tree by Miss Mary house looking good," her father said as they drove past. "Next month going be sweet."

"You remember when Sharon and me used to climb that one?" Gwen smiled at the memory. "Till Miss Mary catch we that time?"

Her father's laugh was warm in the pre-dawn quiet. "She chase all you right down to de crossroads. But next day she still give you both Julie mango."

The road wound down toward town, passing through villages where life was just starting to stir. A woman swept her yard in Keys Village, the brush making soft shushing sounds in the morning stillness. In Conaree, the smell of someone's coal pot breakfast drifted across the road, rich with saltfish and onions.

As they approached town, the sea appeared, still holding the last of night's darkness. Small fishing boats were coming in, their lights tiny stars on the water.

"You want we get some fish?" her father asked, already turning toward the pier. "Fresh catch always good for Sunday cook-up."

The fishermen were unloading their morning's work, the air rich with sea salt and scales. Gwen followed her father to where old Mr. Phipps was sorting his catch.

"Morning Mr. Phipps," her father called. "What de sea give we today?"

"Some good snapper," Mr. Phipps gestured to a pile of red-scaled fish. "Best ones me catch this week."

Her father selected several fish, the haggling more ritual than real between old friends. "Hold these," he told Gwen, passing her the string of fish.

The weight felt familiar in her hands - how many market mornings had she done this? The scales gleamed in the strengthening light as she carried them back to the truck, not flinching when one twitched against her leg. Her father wrapped them carefully in newspaper for the ride home.

The market was filling up when they arrived, regular vendors claiming their usual spots. They set up between Miss Mary with her ground provisions and Mr. Thompson selling his honey, laying out their own offerings - dasheen fresh from their plot, sweet potatoes, yams.

Morning unfolded in the rhythm of sales and greetings. Gwen watched her father transform as he always did on market days, tiredness from factory work falling away as he called out to passing customers, joked with other vendors, explained to tourists the difference between white yam and yellow yam.

"You getting good at this," he said after she handled a particularly picky customer. "Learning when to talk and when to just let people think they discovering something new."

Heat rose in her cheeks at the praise. Then his voice changed, becoming that smooth, slow tone that always made her nervous: "Me hear you been spending plenty time wit some boy lately."

She looked up sharply, but her father was examining a yam with careful attention. She could never tell with that voice - whether he was angry or amused or something else entirely.

"Just..." he paused, still not looking at her. "Some things take their own time to grow right. Like how yam vine can't be rushed."

"Yes, daddy." She understood he wasn't really talking about yams.

The sun climbed higher, burning off the morning cool. They sold most of their provisions - a good enough day to feel satisfied but not enough to celebrate.

"You hungry?" her father asked as they packed up. His voice had changed again, lighter now. "Me hear bout this new place up by de main road. Dem doing something different - pizza they call it."

Gwen's heart jumped. She'd seen pizza on Save by the Bell, the way Lisa and her friends would gather at The Max with their perfect slices, cheese stretching as they laughed about their perfect American school problems. "For true, daddy?"

"Why not? We did good today."

They drove up into the hills where a small wooden hut stood back from the road, draped in red, gold, and green cloth that danced in the breeze. The smell was different from anything Gwen knew - rich and spicy and strange.

Her excitement bubbled as they walked in, her father telling her to order whatever she wanted. But as she read the menu board, her face fell slightly. This wasn't anything like what she'd seen on TV. Instead of the pepperoni and cheese that Lisa would order at The Max, there were things like "Ital Delight" with peas and potatoes, "Garden Blessing" covered in callaloo and pumpkin, "Roots Revival" heavy with dasheen and carrots.

"Different ain't always bad," her father said softly, seeing her expression. "Sometimes the best things in life come when you ain't expecting them."

They ordered something called "Island Inspiration" that came loaded with local vegetables. Gwen smiled and nodded as she ate, pretending each bite was exactly what she'd hoped for. But this wasn't the pizza from Save by the Bell - this was something else entirely, something that belonged to their world of coal pots and provision grounds rather than American diners and high school hallways. Still, seeing her father's enjoyment made her keep eating, hiding her disappointment behind careful smiles.

The drive home traced their morning journey in reverse, but somehow the road always looked different going home, like the day's light showed new truths in familiar places. The fish wrapped in newspaper, the leftover pizza box, and the memory of her father's words about things taking their own time to grow right - all of it felt like pieces of a larger story she was just beginning to understand.

13

The morning bell hadn't rung yet. Gwen stood at the school gate, her fingers tight around her bag strap, watching other students stream past. Sharon paused beside her.

"You sure bout this?" Sharon's voice was low. "Plenty people go see you in you uniform going the wrong way."

"Me know." Gwen's stomach twisted. She'd never skipped school before - none of them had. But something had shifted lately, like the ground wasn't quite solid under her feet anymore.

"Me could tell them you went home sick," Sharon offered.

Gwen shook her head. In St. Kitts, news traveled faster than coconuts rolling downhill. If anyone saw her on a bus heading anywhere instead of towards her home in bed, word would reach her mother before lunch.

She watched Lenwell across the yard, standing with his friends like any other morning. They'd planned it carefully - he would take the first bus. She would wait seven minutes, then catch the next one that went in the same direction. Anyone seeing them would never connect the two journeys.

"You better go through the gate," Sharon said. "Make it look right before you leave."

Gwen nodded, following the crowd through the gates. Her uniform felt like a beacon - everyone knew which school each uniform belonged to, which direction students should be walking. Even now she could feel eyes on her, calculating, wondering.

The first bell rang. Students quickened their pace toward the building. Gwen watched Lenwell slip away from his friends, moving casual like he was just going to the bathroom. Nobody looked twice at him.

She counted to fifty in her head, like they'd planned. Then she turned, walking quick but not too quick back toward the gate. Every step felt like someone would call out, would stop her.

"Gwendolyn?"

She froze. Miss Julie from next door was passing on her way to market.

"You alright, child? You looking pale."

"Just feeling little sick," Gwen managed. "Going home to lay down."

Miss Julie's eyes held something - concern? Suspicion? "You want me walk with you? Me could tell you mother-"

"No!" Too quick. Too loud. She tried again, softer. "No thank you. Me gon be fine."

She watched Miss Julie continue toward's the market, knowing this moment would become conversation over somebody's fence before sunset. But by then...

The bus appeared at the bottom of the hill. She could see Lenwell through the windows, sitting careful casual near the back. As it passed, he didn't look at her.

Seven minutes. She counted every second, feeling exposed in her uniform, imagining her mother's face if she found out, her father's smooth, slow voice asking questions she couldn't answer.

Another bus approached. Her heart thundered as she climbed aboard, coins clutched tight in her sweating palm. The driver didn't look twice at her school uniform - plenty of students took buses home sick. This was certainly normal. wasn't it?

She sank into a seat, keeping her eyes down, thinking about Sharon covering for her, about Miss Julie's knowing look, about all the ways a small island kept its children in line with nothing but watching eyes and waiting tongues.

The bus pulled away from the school. Through the window, she could just see Sharon entering the building, walking the path of the good girl she'd always been until this moment. Something shifted in Gwen's chest - excitement or fear or maybe both, she couldn't tell anymore.

She watched familiar houses pass and fields of sugar cane, everything looking different in this forbidden morning light. Somewhere ahead, another bus carried Lenwell toward whatever this day would become. No turning back now.

14

The bus rattled past Lodge, past Molyneaux, each familiar village making her heart beat faster. She kept her eyes down when other passengers got on, praying nobody would recognize her as Richard's daughter from the factory.

When she finally stepped off in Christ Church, her legs felt weak. Lenwell waited in the shade of a breadfruit tree, looking so sure of himself that something in her chest tightened. How could he be so calm when her whole body trembled?

"You come," he said softly, reaching for her hand. She hesitated, glancing around the quiet village street.

"A frighten," she whispered.

His fingers found hers anyway, warm and steady against her shaking ones. "Me know. But look - nobody here but we two."

They walked through the village, past wooden houses with their neat yards and hanging clothes. Each time someone appeared, Gwen's heart jumped, but Lenwell kept walking like this was the most natural thing in the world - him holding hands with a girl in school uniform in the middle of a Tuesday morning.

"Nobody gon say nothing," he assured her, but she noticed how he led them down the quieter paths, away from the main road where everybody's grandmother had eyes that were sharper than a hawk's.

His house sat back from the road, painted pale yellow with white trim. The front step creaked under their feet as he unlocked the door. The sound seemed to echo in her ears like a warning.

"You sure nobody home?" Her voice came out smaller than she meant it to.

"Me fadda deh a wuk till late. Me mudda at she sister in Sandy Point till weekend." His voice held that same certainty that had gotten them here, but now it had a deeper note that made her shiver.

Inside smelled of clean laundry and something cooking slow - maybe food that was cooked earlier and left to cool. Normal, everyday smells that somehow made everything feel more real.

He led her down a narrow hallway to his room. The floor sloped slightly, making her step down into the space like entering somewhere separate from the rest of the house. Something about that dip in the floor made her pause - like crossing this threshold meant crossing something bigger.

"We no have to..." he started, seeing her hesitation.

"Me no know what we supposed to do," she admitted.

His room felt both exactly like she'd imagined and completely different - the neat bed with its blue and white striped sheets, a desk with schoolbooks stacked careful, football and cricket trophies lined up on a shelf, the window letting in strips of sunlight through the spaces in the curtains.

He pulled her close, gentle like she might break. Her hands found his shoulders, feeling the strength there beneath his school shirt. Their faces drew closer, breaths mixing in the quiet space.

"Tell me if you want me stop," he whispered.

But when his lips met hers, stopping was the last thing on her mind. This kiss was different from their careful ones behind the wooden house - deeper, like he was trying to tell her something his words couldn't say. Her fingers curled into his shirt as he pulled her closer, their bodies fitting together like they'd been made that way.

They ended up on his bed without really meaning to, the blue and white sheets cool against her heated skin. Everything felt dream-like - the way sunlight striped across them through the curtains, how his weight beside her made the mattress dip, pulling her toward him like gravity.

His hands stayed respectful but wanting, tracing patterns that made her shiver. Their uniforms stayed on but became maps of wrinkles that told stories of touches and almost-touches. Each moment brought them closer to something neither was quite ready for, but couldn't quite resist either.

"A got to go," she whispered finally, though her body protested every word.

The walk to the bus stop felt like walking through molasses, everything slow and sweet and heavy. Neither spoke much - what could they say about what had almost happened, what might happen next time?

The ride home seemed to take forever and no time at all. Her uniform smelled like him now, like secrets and promises and things she did not know how to name. But as the bus carried her closer to home, she found herself already thinking about how to make it back to that sloping floor, those blue and white sheets, those kisses that felt like falling.

15

E very look felt suspicious. Jennifer's too-long stare during morning assembly. The way Mr. Pemberton paused at her desk during Geography. Even the woman at the pink house seemed to study her longer than usual while serving the rice and stew.

"Girl, you looking guilty," Sharon whispered during afternoon break. "People gon know something up if you keep jumping every time somebody look at you."

"You think anybody know?"

"Me no hear nothing yet." Sharon leaned closer. "But you gon tell me what happen or what?"

Before Gwen could answer, a group of girls passed by, their whispers carrying just enough for Gwen to catch "...uniform..." and "...Christ Church..." Her stomach clenched.

"Them talking bout netball," Sharon said quickly. "Game against Christ Church next week. You too jumpy."

But Gwen couldn't shake the feeling that everyone knew, that they could somehow see yesterday written all over her face. She kept remembering the sloping floor of Lenwell's room, the blue and white sheets, his hands...

"Wake up yuhself, Gwen!" Sharon's voice snapped her back. "You ain't even hear what me say."

"Sorry. Just..."

"Just thinking bout certain somebody room?" Sharon's grin faded at Gwen's sharp look. "Alright, alright. But you gon have to tell me something eventually."

The walk home started normal enough. She and Sharon parted at their usual corner, making plans for tomorrow like any other day. But as Gwen rounded the bend toward her house, she stopped short.

Ms. Netty stood at her gate, talking to her parents in that serious way teachers had when they came to your house. The last time she'd seen that look was when she'd gotten in trouble for fighting with Mikey in third form. She'd hated then how their teacher lived close enough to just stop by and how nothing in a small place ever stayed secret for long.

Her mother noticed her first. "Gwendolyn! Come here right now!"

She forced her feet to move, each step feeling heavier than the last. Her father's face held that unreadable expression she dreaded, while her mother's cheeks were flushed with anger.

"You want tell we where you been yesterday?" Her mother's voice rose sharply. "Because according to you teacher-"

The cough started suddenly, cutting off her words. Not her usual gentle cough, but something deeper, harder. Her mother grabbed the gate for support, but her legs seemed to buckle.

"Martha!" Her father moved quickly, catching her mother before she fell. Ms. Netty stepped forward to help, all thoughts of Gwen's misdeeds forgotten for the moment.

"Me fine," her mother tried to say between coughs. "Just need..." But she couldn't finish, her breathing arrived in sharp gasps that seemed to tear through the afternoon quiet.

They half-carried her inside, leaving Gwen frozen at the gate. Through the window, she could see her mother being settled in her kitchen chair, her father's hands gentle but shaking as he held a glass of water to her lips. Ms. Netty hovered nearby, her teacher-stern face replaced by genuine concern.

Gwen stood outside, the weight of everything pressing down on her - the secret of yesterday, the look on her father's face, but most of all the sound of her mother's cough echoing in her ears. The same cough she'd been trying not to notice getting worse for weeks now.

She didn't know which was worse - the trouble she was in, or the fear she saw in her father's eyes as he tended to her mother. Both felt like worlds cracking open, revealing depths she wasn't ready to face.

16

Her mother lay in bed, chest slathered with Vicks, the sharp medicinal smell mixing with cerasee tea Miss Mary brewed. Miss Mary came over as soon as she heard the coughing, bringing her special mix of bush tea that everybody swore could cure anything.

"You mudda just need rest," Miss Mary had insisted earlier, showing Gwen how much honey to add to the tea. Not that it mattered - everyone knew Gwen couldn't be trusted near anything involving heat or ingredients. Three burnt pots and one almost-fire had proved that well enough.

The house had quieted now. Miss Mary gone home, her mother sleeping fitfully under a thin sheet despite the heat. Every few minutes, a cough rattled through the walls, making Gwen's chest tight with worry.

She sat in the kitchen, waiting. The smooth, slow voice would come. Just didn't know when.

Her father's heavy steps moved from the bedroom to the kitchen, each footfall carrying the weight of things unsaid. He'd changed out of his factory clothes but still carried that sweet-sharp scent of sugar and machinery that followed him everywhere. When he sat across from her, the kitchen felt smaller somehow.

"You mother sleeping now," he said finally. "That coughing take all she strength."

Gwen nodded, hands clasped tight in her lap.

"So maybe now we could talk bout why Ms. Netty come by we house. Why she tell me somebody see me daughter, me only child, getting off bus in Christ Church when she supposed to be in school."

She stared at her hands, unable to meet his eyes.

"You think me stupid?" His voice stayed level, controlled, but she could hear the hurt beneath it. "You think me no see how that boy looking at you? How you been different lately?"

"He name Lenwell," she whispered.

"He name don't matter. What matter is me daughter think is okay to leave school, go God knows where-"

"We just talk," she said quickly, but felt her face heat with the half-truth.

"Talk?" Now his voice held something dangerous. "Girl, you think me no been young once? You think me no know what kind of 'talk' boy want with girl when nobody watching?"

A knock at the back door interrupted them. Sharon's voice carried through: "Gwen? You there? Me hear bout you mudda."

Her father's eyes held hers. "Go tell she you can't come out. Tell she you in trouble."

Gwen moved to the door, opening it just enough to see her friend's worried face in the gathering evening dark.

"A can't," she said softly. "A in trouble."

"You mudda okay though?"

"She resting. Miss Mary bring bush tea."

"Me could come in? Just for little bit?" Sharon's voice dropped lower. "He outside waiting, you know. Want know what happen."

Gwen's heart jumped, but her father's voice came from behind her: "Sharon could come visit tomorrow if she want. But right now, we dealing with family business."

Sharon nodded, understanding everything unsaid. "Alright. Me see you at school then." She paused, then added so only Gwen could hear, "He say him gon wait long as it take."

The click of the door closing echoed in Gwen's chest. She turned back to her father, who still sat at the kitchen table, his presence filling the small space.

"You me daughter," he said, voice softening slightly. "Me only girl child. You think any father want see he daughter sneaking round with boy? Going places she no supposed to go?"

"But daddy-"

"No. Listen good now. You mother in there sick. Getting worse every day though she no want nobody notice." His words hit her like stones. "Me got factory work, trying to keep food on table, trying to watch you mother getting weaker and weaker. Me no got no strength to be worrying bout where you be and what you doing with some boy."

Through the thin walls, another cough rattled the silence. They both turned toward the sound, waiting until it settled.

"From today," he continued, "you coming straight home after school. No stopping nowhere. No talking to that boy." He held up his hand when she started to protest. "Sharon could come here if she want see you. At least me know what kind of trouble she leading you into. But that boy?" He shook his head. "He got one thing on he mind, and it ain't you future."

"You no even know him," she whispered, feeling tears burn behind her eyes.

"Me know he a boy. Me know how boy think. And me know me daughter worth more than becoming somebody story round town."

She thought about sloping floors and blue and white sheets, about the way Lenwell's hands had trembled when he touched her face. About how he'd said he wanted to do things right. But how could she explain that to her father? How could she make him understand that maybe this wasn't just some boy and some girl, but something more?

"Daddy-"

"Don't." That single word held years of protection, of love, of fear. "Don't make me have to choose between watching you mother and watching you. Because you know which one got to come first."

Another cough from the bedroom, longer this time. Her father stood, moving to check on her mother, but paused in the doorway.

"You me heart, Gwendolyn," he said softly. "But right now you breaking it."

She sat alone in the kitchen as darkness settled fully around their small house. Somewhere out there, Lenwell was waiting, probably standing in the shadows of the mango trees that lined their street. Her heart pulled toward him even as her body stayed rooted to the kitchen chair, held there by duty and love and fear.

The rubber band inside her stretched tighter. Something would have to break eventually. She just didn't know what - or who - it would be.

17

Three days of straight home after school had nearly broken her. Three days of watching her mother try to hide her coughing, of her father coming home smelling of factory and worry, of seeing Lenwell in the schoolyard but having to turn away.

Sharon passed notes between them when she could, but it wasn't the same. "He say he coming to talk to you fadda," she whispered during lunch break. "He want do things right."

"Me fadda go kill him," Gwen said, but something warm bloomed in her chest at the thought of Lenwell wanting to face her father.

The afternoon bell rang too soon, sending her trudging home like every other day this week. But today felt different. Her mother's coughing had gotten worse despite Miss Mary's bush tea, despite the Vicks rubbed thick enough to make the whole house smell like medicine.

She found her mother in the kitchen, trying to stand at the stove.

"What you doing?" Gwen rushed forward as her mother swayed slightly.

"Somebody got to cook," her mother said, voice rough from coughing. "You fadda can't live on bread and butter forever."

"Let me help-"

"Help?" Her mother managed a weak laugh that turned into a cough. "Last time you help, we almost lose we house to fire."

"Then rest. Please. Me could walk up to Miss Mary, ask she-"

A knock at the front door cut her off. Not the back door where Sharon usually came, but the formal front door that nobody ever used. Through the window, Gwen saw him before her mother did - Lenwell, standing straight and proper in his school uniform like he had every right to be there.

"Who that?" Her mother's voice sharpened despite her weakness.

"Nobody," Gwen said quickly. "Probably somebody lost-"

But Lenwell knocked again, more firmly this time. Her mother moved toward the door, each step careful but determined.

"Mammy, no-"

Too late. The door opened, and there stood Lenwell, looking somehow both terrified and certain.

"Good afternoon, Mrs. Richards," he said, his voice steady despite the fear Gwen could see in his eyes. "Me come to speak with you and Mr. Richards. About you daughter."

Her mother's hand tightened on the doorframe, whether from weakness or surprise, Gwen couldn't tell. "Me husband ain't home yet."

"Me could wait." He stood his ground. "This important."

A cough shook her mother then, hard enough that she had to lean against the door. Gwen moved forward to help, but her mother waved her away.

"You the boy from Christ Church," her mother said when she could speak again. "The one who got me daughter skipping school."

"Yes ma'am. That why me here. To say sorry and-"

"You hear that coughing?" Her mother's voice was harder than Gwen had ever heard it. "That what worry keeping inside you chest sound like. That what happen when you watch you only child throwing she self away on boy who think he man enough to come to we house."

"Mammy-"

"Go inside, Gwendolyn."

"But-"

"Now."

Gwen had never heard that tone from her mother before. She backed away, watching through the window as her mother straightened to her full height despite the weakness clearly pulling at her.

"You listen good," she heard her mother say to Lenwell. "Me no got no strength to be fighting with hard-head children right now. Me daughter got more important things to think bout than some boy."

"Yes miss, but-"

"No but. You see that girl? She all me got. All her fadda got. And right now..." Another cough caught her, and Gwen saw Lenwell's hand twitch like he wanted to help. But her mother recovered, voice stronger now. "Right now she need to be thinking bout she future. Not bout some boy who think he could come to we house without invitation."

Through the window, Gwen watched Lenwell's shoulders drop slightly. But he didn't back away.

"Me understand," he said softly. "But me no just some boy. And Gwen no just some girl."

Her mother's laugh was bitter. "That what every young person think. That them different, them special." She coughed again, harder. "Come back in ten years if you still feel so. Right now, all you just pickney playin' big people games."

The coughing wouldn't stop this time. Gwen rushed forward as her mother's knees buckled, barely catching her before she hit the ground. Lenwell moved to help but froze at her mother's glare.

"Go home, boy," her mother managed between coughs. "Go home before her fadda find you here."

Gwen met his eyes over her mother's shaking shoulders. Something passed between them - fear, love, determination - before he turned and walked away, his back straight despite the defeat.

She managed to get her mother to bed, the coughing eventually easing into ragged breaths. But something had changed. Gwen could feel it in the air, in the way her mother's hand clutched hers before letting go.

"You think you in love," her mother whispered. "But love no supposed to make you forget who you is, who you family is."

Gwen said nothing, just adjusted the sheet over her mother's shoulders.

"Promise me," her mother's voice faded as sleep pulled at her. "Promise me you no go throw you life away on some boy."

But Gwen couldn't make that promise. Not when her heart lived outside her body now, walking home in a school uniform, probably already planning his next attempt to prove himself worthy.

18

The radio crackled with same ominous voice reading out the morning's death announcements while Gwen helped her mother to the kitchen table. These days, every movement seemed to take twice the effort, like her mother's body was becoming heavier while growing smaller at the same time.

"Gwen!" Sharon's voice carried from outside. "We late!"

"Go on," her mother said, waving her away. "Me gon be fine."

But Gwen hesitated, watching her mother's hands shake as she reached for her tea cup. Three weeks had passed since Lenwell's visit to their door, since her mother's coughing fit had scared them all. Three weeks of watching, waiting,

pretending not to notice how each day brought new worries.

"Gwendolyn!" This time it was her father's voice from
his bedroom. "You hear Sharon calling you?"

She grabbed her bag, pressing a quick kiss to her mother's cheek before rushing out. Sharon waited at the gate,
knowing better than to come inside these days.

"He say he got a plan," Sharon whispered as they walked.
"Tonight."

Gwen's heart jumped. She hadn't spoken to Lenwell
properly since that day at her door, but she'd felt his eyes
following her in school, had caught the meaning in his
glances.

"What kind of plan?"

"He say wait by you window after everybody sleep. He
know which one it is from watching you house all this
time."

"A can't." But even as she said it, something inside her
pulled toward the idea. "If me fadda catch me..."

"Then don't let him catch you."

They reached the school gates where Lenwell stood with
his friends, looking like any other boy on any other morn-

ing. But when his eyes met hers, that same electricity from his bedroom jumped between them.

The day crawled. Every class felt longer than the last, every minute stretching like molasses in the afternoon heat. During last period, a note appeared on her desk: "11 o'clock. Just for a little while."

She thought about her father's smooth voice, her mother's shaking hands, all the reasons she should burn this note and forget about boys with plans and night time promises. But when night fell and the house quieted, she found herself lying awake, fully dressed under her covers, listening to her father's snores and her mother's labored breathing from the next room.

The knock came so soft she almost missed it. Three tiny taps against her window glass.

Her hands shook as she eased the window open. Lenwell stood in the shadows of the mango tree that grew close to the house, its branches making perfect hiding spots.

"You coming?" he whispered.

Looking at him in the darkness, everything felt possible. She glanced back at her closed door, thinking about promises and obligations and the weight of being somebody's only daughter. Then she looked at Lenwell again, at the future she could see in his eyes.

The window ledge wasn't high. One quick movement and she'd be outside, free, his hand already reaching for hers...

A harsh cough from her parents' room made her freeze. Through the thin walls, she heard her father's voice, gentle in a way he never was with anyone else: "Martha? You need water?"

"Go back sleep," her mother's voice came weak, thread-like. "Me fine."

But the coughing continued, each sound like stones dropping in Gwen's stomach. She looked at Lenwell, saw the understanding dawn in his eyes even before she shook her head.

"Me can't," she whispered. "Not tonight."

He nodded, but didn't move away. "Tomorrow?"

Another cough rattled through the house. Her father's footsteps moved toward the kitchen, probably to make tea.

"Me no know," she said honestly. "But..."

"But you want to."

It wasn't a question. They both knew the truth of it, knew that something had started that couldn't be stopped, only delayed.

"Go," she whispered as her father's footsteps returned to the bedroom. "Before somebody see you."

He melted into the darkness like he'd never been there. But as Gwen lay in bed later, still fully dressed, listening to her mother's coughing finally ease into uneasy sleep, she knew things couldn't stay this way. Something had to break - her father's rules, her mother's health, her own heart. She just didn't know which would break first.

19

The coughing didn't stop that night. Gwen lay awake listening to her mother's struggle for air, her father's quiet words of comfort, the sound of feet moving back and forth to the kitchen for water. When dawn finally came, painting the mango tree outside her window with first light, she heard her father's voice, tight with worry.

"Martha, we got to go hospital."

"No." Her mother's voice came between coughs. "You know how people who go hospital-"

"Just for them check you proper," he said quickly. "In and out. Like when Gwen did break she arm that time."

But they all knew breaking an arm was different. People who went to hospital for things inside them, things that made breathing hard and strength fade - those people didn't always come back out.

The morning air hung thick with coal pot smoke and the scent of someone's johnny cakes cooking next door. Normal smells that made everything feel wrong - how could the world keep going when her mother could barely stand?

"Me could drive the Bug," her father said, already helping her mother dress. "So you don't have to climb up in a de truck."

Miss Mary appeared without being called, the way neighbors did in times of trouble. She moved around their kitchen gathering things they might need while Gwen stood useless in her doorway, still in her nightdress.

"You go get ready for school," her father said, his voice holding that smooth, slow quality that meant no arguments. "Everything go be fine. Just routine check."

But nothing felt routine about helping her mother into the old VW Bug, watching each breath shake her thin shoulders. Her father's hands gripped the steering wheel too tight, his knuckles white against the black plastic.

"Me coming back tonight after work," he said, his voice rough. "Sharon mother say she go bring food."

Gwen nodded, not trusting her voice. The Bug pulled away, carrying her mother down the road that wound toward Basseterre. She stood at the gate long after it disappeared, listening to the morning sounds of Lodge waking up - somebody's goat complaining, a neighbor's radio playing old reggae, the distant horn of the sugar factory calling workers to their shift.

School felt impossible, but she went anyway. Her father would expect it. The uniform felt stiff and wrong, like she was playing at normal life while everything crumbled.

"You alright?" Sharon asked when they met at their corner.

She shook her head. Words seemed too hard.

Their classroom filled with the usual morning noise, but Gwen barely noticed. Teachers came and went, their voices washing over her like waves while she stared at her mother's empty space in her mind. Even when Lenwell caught her eye from across the room, she could barely focus on his worried look.

The day passed in a blur of teachers rotating through their classroom, lessons she couldn't absorb, and Sharon's quiet presence beside her. When final bell rang, she shouldered her bag to head home to an empty house, but felt a touch on her arm.

"Let me walk with you," Lenwell said softly.

She should've said no. Should've gone straight home like her father expected. But the thought of that quiet house, no smell of cooking, no sound of her mother's movements...

They took the long way, past the sugarcane fields that swayed in the breeze, past the football field where younger children played after school, through the shortcut by the old cricket ground where bougainvillea spilled over fences in bright cascades of pink and purple. Neither spoke until they reached the edge of Lodge.

"A wish a could do something," he said finally.

"Is nothing nobody could do." Her voice caught. "Just got to wait."

He reached for her hand. She should've pulled away - anybody could see them here. But his fingers were warm and solid when everything else felt like it might disappear.

At her gate, he squeezed her hand once before letting go. "A gon be here. Whatever you need."

She watched him walk away, his school shirt bright in the afternoon sun. The house waited, silent and strange.

Inside, signs of the morning's rush still showed - her mother's favorite cup unwashed in the sink, the jar of Vicks open on the counter, a blackened johnny cake (her father's first attempt at cooking) sitting untouched on a plate.

The quiet pressed in until she couldn't stand it. She turned on the radio just to hear another voice. The evening death announcements played their familiar rhythm, but she barely registered the names—just another part of the ritual, like the lowing of cattle in the distance or the restless shuffle of goats searching for a cool place to settle.

Evening brought Sharon's mother with food - rice and stew chicken still hot from her stove. "You fadda say he working late shift," she said, setting down the pot. "He go come check you after."

But the factory whistle had blown its last shift hours ago, and still he hadn't come. Gwen knew he was at the hospital, probably sitting in one of those hard chairs outside the ward since visiting hours were done, unable to leave, unable to help.

She lay in bed that night listening to all the sounds that weren't there - no coughing from the next room, no murmur of her parents' voices, no familiar creak of floorboards under her mother's steps. Just the night breeze moving through mango leaves outside her window, and somewhere in the distance, a dog barking at the moon.

Her window faced the direction of Basseterre. Somewhere out there, her mother lay in a hospital bed. Somewhere in another direction, Lenwell was probably thinking of her too. The thought shouldn't have comforted her, but it did.

20

Three days of hospital visits had worn tracks in their lives - her father's Bug leaving before dawn, returning after dark, the truck sitting idle in the yard like it too was waiting for normal life to return. Even the sugar factory's whistle seemed to blow differently, like it felt the absence of routine.

"You mother go come home soon," Sharon said during lunch break, the only time they could talk freely in their classroom. "Me grandmudda say you mudda dem people strong like Brimstone Hill."

Gwen nodded, picking at the cold beef patty Sharon had shared with her. These days, nobody thought to give her lunch money - her father barely remembered to take care of himself.

Lenwell sat with his friends across the room, but she felt his eyes on her between bites, between conversations. His presence anchored her when everything else felt adrift.

"You walking home?" he asked as their last teacher gathered his books. His voice was casual, but something in it tugged at her, warm as afternoon sun.

She should say no. Her father could come home early, could skip his evening hospital visit. But the thought of another silent afternoon in that empty house made her chest tighten.

"Me got to go home and help me mudda," Sharon said, but her eyes held understanding. "You go ahead."

They took the track that ran alongside the cane fields, where the afternoon sun turned everything to gold. The cane stood tall and proud, ready for cutting season, their blades whispering in the breeze.

A narrow path led off the main track, worn by cane cutters who'd already headed home for the day. Without discussing it, they turned onto it, letting the tall cane close around them. Here, the world narrowed to just them and the cane - no hospital worries, no empty house, no father's tired eyes.

"Me used to cut through here when me was small," Lenwell said, his voice soft in their private world. "Before them tell we bout crapo and centipede."

"You wasn't 'fraid?"

"Maybe little bit." He grinned. "But sometimes the quickest way home go straight through what you 'fraid of."

They reached a small clearing where the cane formed natural walls around them. Old cuttings lay scattered - the cutters must've used this spot for their break time. Lenwell bent to pick up a piece of fallen cane, young and fresh enough to still be good.

His hands moved with the sureness of island children who grew up knowing sugar cane's secrets. The blade fell away under his thumbnail, revealing the pale sweetness inside. But instead of stripping it fully like last time, he broke off a small piece and held it out to her.

"Here," he said simply.

They sat in the clearing, the dry cane trash crackling beneath them, passing the piece back and forth, working their way through its segments. The ritual of it felt ancient somehow - how many couples before them had shared cane's sweetness in hidden places like this?

"You mudda go be alright," he said after a while, his shoulder warm against hers.

"You no know that?"

"Me know you. Know you come from strong people." His fingers found hers, sticky with cane juice. "Like how cane grow strong no matter what weather come."

She looked at their joined hands, brown sugar against brown sugar, sweet with the same sweetness. His thumb traced patterns on her palm that made her skin tingle.

When he kissed her, she tasted sugar and sunshine and something deeper - want maybe, or need. The cane stood tall around them, guardian of their secrets, while distant sounds drifted by - a goat bleating, children playing somewhere beyond their hidden world, the regular rhythm of island life continuing despite everything.

His hand cupped her face, gentle like she might break. "We got to be careful," he whispered, but didn't move away.

"Me know." But she leaned closer anyway, letting herself forget about hospitals and worried fathers and empty houses. Just for now, just for this moment, while the sun hung low enough to paint the cane tops golden and time seemed to slow like molasses in July.

They shared another piece of cane, their movements slower now, more deliberate. Each brush of fingers felt charged with something new, something that both scared and thrilled her. The sweet juice couldn't quite wash away the taste of his kiss, not that she wanted it to.

But too soon, the sun's angle changed, warning them of time passed. They emerged from the cane field separately - him first, then her a few minutes later. Her uniform would need pressing, and sugar cane always left its mark, but she couldn't bring herself to regret it.

Miss Mary stood at her fence like she'd been waiting, though her eyes held more understanding than judgment. "You fadda call from hospital," she said. "Say he coming home early tonight. Say you mudda resting good."

Inside, Gwen tried to straighten her uniform, to wash away the evidence of stolen sweetness. But some things couldn't be hidden - the flush in her cheeks, the memory of Lenwell's hands, the way her heart still raced thinking of how close they'd sat, how easy it would be to let things go further.

The factory whistle blew its end-of-shift song. Soon her father would return, smelling of machinery and hospital corridors. She touched her lips, still feeling the ghost of sugar and kisses there. Tomorrow they'd have to be more careful. Tomorrow she'd have to be the good daughter again.

But for now, she let herself remember how it felt to be held, to be wanted, to taste sweetness in a bitter time. The cane field rustled in the evening breeze, keeping her secrets safe behind its green and gold walls.

21

Her father stood at the stove, stirring a pot of something that actually smelled good. These days he moved slower, weighted by factory work and hospital visits, but his hands stayed steady as he added seasonings without measuring.

"Taste this," he said, holding out the wooden spoon. The stew had just the right amount of salt, thyme singing through the rich broth. "You mudda teach me this one long time, before you was born."

The phone rang before Gwen could respond.

Turning away from the pot, her father answered.

"They say she resting better today," he said after hanging up. "But me still going after we eat. Just for little bit."

The Bug's engine faded into evening quiet an hour later. Through her window, Gwen watched porch lights clicking on up and down their street, the scent of different suppers drifting between houses - curry from the Salters next door, somebody's fresh baked bread, someone else's frying fish.

The phone rang again. Sharon's voice came through excited: "Hold on, a got somebody want talk to you."

A click, then silence. Another click.

"You there?" Sharon's voice again.

"Yeah."

"He there too. Me go connect all we."

One more click, then Lenwell's voice, soft and sure: "You there, Gwen?"

Her heart jumped at the sound. Sharon's end went quiet - not hanging up, just listening like they always did on three-way calls.

"Yes." She twisted the phone cord around her finger, suddenly nervous.

"You by yourself?"

She should've lied. Should've said Miss Mary, or anybody. Instead: "Yes."

"You want company? A could catch de bus..."

"Somebody go see you."

"Not if me careful." A pause. "You shouldn't be by you-self every night."

She looked around the empty house, at her father's clean dishes drying by the sink, at her mother's empty chair. "Me no know..."

"Just to talk. Please?"

The please undid her. Sharon's end stayed quiet, but Gwen could feel her friend listening, protecting.

"Alright," she whispered. "But you got to be careful."

She spent the next hour straightening things that didn't need straightening, jumping at every passing car sound. The faint rap at the door was so delicate it nearly melted into the hush of the evening.

Her heart thundered as she opened the door, certain every neighbor must've heard it. But the street lay quiet, houses turned inward to their evening routines. Lenwell slipped inside bringing with him the smell of evening air and bus ride dust.

They stood awkward in the front room, all their easy cane field comfort forgotten in this new space. Her mother's photographs watched from the walls - wedding pictures, family gatherings, church portraits lined up neat and proper.

"You want..." She gestured vaguely toward the kitchen, then stopped, remembering all the times her mother had warned about boys and empty houses.

But Lenwell just nodded, following her to the kitchen where her father's stew still warmed on the stove. "Smell good," he said, then: "You want me go? You looking nervous."

"No." The word came quick, surprising them both. "J ust... nobody ever come visit me like this before."

His smile was soft in the kitchen light. "Nobody ever want visit anybody like this before."

They eased into their seats at the kitchen table, the conversation flowing more naturally, like a river finding its course. He told her about his sister's new baby, about his father's promotion at the factory office, about normal things that made the world feel steady again. She found herself laughing for the first time in days.

As his fingers lightly grazed hers across the worn wooden table, the laughter between them stilled, giving way to something deeper, more electric. The kitchen, once spacious and filled with the scent of simmering spices, seemed to shrink around them, wrapping them in an intimate warmth. The air thickened, charged with unspoken words and lingering glances. His touch, fleeting yet deliberate, whispered promises neither dared to voice, a silent confession that neither of them was quite ready to acknowledge.

"Me shouldn't stay too long," he said, but didn't move away.

"Little bit longer?" Her voice came out softer than she intended, the quiet plea hanging between them like a delicate thread.

His gaze lingered on her lips before he closed the space between them. When he kissed her, it wasn't like their stolen moments in the cane fields, all breathless urgency and secrecy. This was slower, deeper—weighted with the knowledge that, for once, they weren't looking over their shoulders. The house held its breath around them, the empty chair at the table a silent witness. His hands traced the curve of her back, pulling her closer until the warmth of him drowned out everything else. The world outside could wait.

Each touch felt like a question and an answer both. His fingers trailed fire along her jawline, down her neck, making her shiver despite the evening heat.

A car passed outside, headlights sweeping across the kitchen window. They jumped apart, hearts racing, but it was just someone heading home, unaware of the moment they'd interrupted.

"Me really should go," he said, his voice rough with something new.

At the door, he turned back, his fingers finding hers one last time. No words needed - they both felt it, this thing growing between them like cane reaching for sun.

"Tomorrow?"

She nodded, not trusting her voice. After he disappeared into the darkness, she stood watching until she couldn't hear his footsteps anymore. The night air carried the last traces of cooking smells, the sound of someone's TV through an open window, normal life going on while something inside her shifted like sand under waves.

The kitchen still held the warmth of his presence, the memory of his touch. She pressed her fingers to where his had been, remembering how close they'd come to letting comfort become something else. How easy it would have been to let him stay longer next time, to find solace in his arms while the world changed around them.

The thought should have scared her. Instead, it felt as natural as rain falling in September, as inevitable as the tide pulling at the shore, as unstoppable as tomorrow coming whether they were ready or not.

22

Night settled different when you were alone. Every sound echoed louder - the hum of the fridge, a neighbor's TV, the occasional car passing. Gwen moved through the quiet house, straightening things already straight, checking the clock that seemed stuck between minutes.

Her father had called hours ago. "Them doctor want to do more test," he'd said, his voice heavy with something he wasn't saying. "You go eat something?"

She'd lied, said yes, though Sharon's mother's food sat untouched in the kitchen. The weight in the air pressed down, making even breathing feel like work.

The phone rang again just past eight. Sharon's voice came through first: "You alright?"

"Yeah." But they both heard the lie.

"Hold on," Sharon said. "Somebody want talk to you."

The familiar clicks of three-way, then Lenwell's voice soft with concern: "You fadda still deh a hospital?"

"Yeah." She sank into her mother's chair, twisting the phone cord until her finger turned white. "He say doctor want talk to him."

Silence stretched between them, heavy with understanding. Then: "You shouldn't be by you-self tonight."

She pressed her forehead against her knees, fighting tears. "Me done cry too much already."

"Let me come." His voice gentled further. "Just to sit with you."

She should say no. Should be the good daughter, especially now. Instead: "Alright."

Sharon's end stayed quiet, protective. "Me go stay on phone till he reach," she said finally.

The wait stretched like sugar boiling in a copper pot, thick and slow, promising something sweet but making them suffer for it. Minutes dragged while Sharon talked about nothing and everything - school gossip, her little brother's latest trouble, normal things that made the world feel almost right.

Then a soft knock. "He here," Gwen whispered.

"You want me stay on?"

"No. But... thanks."

"Call if you need anything. No matter what time."

Lenwell stood in the doorway looking like everything solid in a world gone soft at the edges. He'd changed from his school clothes into a clean shirt that gleamed white in the porch light.

No words passed between them as she let him in. None were needed. His arms opened and she fell into them like rain finding earth, like waves finding shore, like all the pieces of herself she'd been holding together finally breaking apart.

They ended up on the sofa, her tears soaking his clean shirt while his hands moved gentle over her back, her hair, her face. When she lifted her head, his eyes held everything she couldn't say.

The first kiss tasted of salt and need. The second of comfort and want mixed together until she couldn't tell which was which. His hands shook as they traced paths along her skin that left fire in their wake.

"We could stop," he whispered against her neck.

She answered by pulling him closer, letting actions speak what words couldn't reach. Time dissolved into sensation—the softness of his touch against her bare shoulders, the way moonlight painted silver paths across their skin, how the night air moved warm through open windows.

Pain flared, brief and sharp, a stinging reminder of firsts, but his gentleness turned it to something else, something that made her forget everything but this moment, this feeling, this boy who held her like she was precious, breakable, and strong all at once.

"You good?" he asked after, his voice rough with emotion she'd never heard before.

She nodded against his chest, feeling fundamentally changed yet somehow more herself than ever. Outside, life continued its nighttime rhythm - dogs conversing across yards, the last bus grumbling past, someone's radio playing old reggae soft enough to barely hear.

The sound of tires on gravel shattered their bubble. Headlights swung across the ceiling - her father's Bug turning into the drive.

Terror shot through her body. "Quick," she whispered. "De back door."

They scrambled for clothes, panic making their fingers clumsy. Lenwell slipped out just as the front door opened, taking with him the last moments of her childhood innocence.

She tried to straighten her dress, to smooth her hair, to look like her world hadn't just shifted on two different axes. But when she turned, the look on her father's face froze everything inside her.

The kitchen chair scraped against the floor as he sank into it. All the strength seemed to have left his body, leaving just a shell of the man who'd left that morning.

"Gwendolyn." That smooth voice cracked on her name. "Come here, child."

The walk from doorway to table felt endless. Each step carried her closer to news she already knew but couldn't face. His hands shook as they found hers, and in that tremor she read everything.

"You mudda..." He stopped, swallowed hard. "De doctors say..."

The world tilted sideways. She felt herself falling, felt her father's arms catch her like they had a thousand times before, felt his tears wet against her hair as they held each other in the wreckage of their broken family.

Outside, cars still passed. Dogs still barked. The world kept turning like it didn't know everything had just ended. But in their kitchen, time stopped. Her father's arms were the only thing keeping her from shattering completely as guilt and grief tangled together in her chest until she couldn't tell where one ended and the other began.

23

Morning arrived in whispers. Miss Mary's voice carried through the kitchen window first, speaking low with someone in the yard. Then more voices joined, a quiet chorus of neighbors gathering as news traveled the way it did in small places - faster than light, carried on concerned tongues and worried hearts.

Gwen lay in her bed, watching sunrise paint familiar shadows on her ceiling. Her school uniform hung ready on the door, but school seemed like something from another life now. Every breath felt heavy, weighted with the knowledge that her mother would never again call her for breakfast, never fuss about her homework, never do any of the thousand small things that made up their daily life.

Her father's footsteps moved through the house, answering another knock at the door. She heard Miss Mary's voice again: "Me bring food. And Sister Jenkins making she special bread. Whole church go be here soon."

The bed seemed to hold her like quicksand, each movement requiring more strength than she possessed. But another knock echoed through the house, and another, the sound of community arriving with food and prayers and practiced words of comfort.

When she finally managed to stand, her reflection in the mirror stopped her. Same face as yesterday, but different somehow. The girl who'd given herself to Lenwell in desperate passion, and the girl who'd lost her mother hours later - they stared back at her from the same eyes, making her stomach twist with guilt and grief and things she couldn't name.

The hallway stretched longer than usual, each step carrying her past photographs that felt like accusations - her mother's wedding picture, family portraits from christenings and Christmas, moments frozen in time that would never come again.

Their front room had transformed overnight into a gathering place. Women moved with practiced efficiency, setting out dishes, arranging chairs, speaking in the hushed tones reserved for houses of mourning. The air filled with the scent of fresh bread and lemongrass tea, of familiar foods brought by knowing hands.

Her father sat at the kitchen table, looking smaller somehow in daylight. Papers spread before him - forms and documents, the bureaucracy of death that couldn't wait for grief. Miss Mary stood at his shoulder, her voice gentle but firm as she helped him navigate the necessary arrangements.

"Gwen." Sharon appeared from nowhere, solid and real when everything else felt dream-like. She didn't offer empty words, just wrapped her arms around Gwen and held on while the world spun beneath their feet.

More people arrived. Aunts who lived in town, cousins from the country, neighbors who were close as blood. Each brought food, each touched Gwen's shoulder or hands with gentle sympathy, each added their presence to the growing crowd that filled their small house with murmured prayers and memories.

"You mudda was good woman," Sister Jenkins said, pressing a still-warm loaf of bread into Gwen's hands. "Strong in faith, strong in love. She raise you right."

The words scraped against Gwen's conscience. If only they knew what she'd done last night while her mother lay dying. The thought sent her stumbling toward the back door, needing air that didn't smell of other people's sympathy.

The morning sun felt wrong on her skin, too bright for a world without her mother in it. Their small yard had filled with more people arriving, carrying covered dishes and speaking in low voices. Through the crowd, she caught a glimpse of Lenwell standing at the edge of the road, uncertainty written in every line of his body.

Their eyes met across the space. In his face she saw everything - love, guilt, grief, worry - reflecting her own turbulent emotions back at her. But before either could move, her father's voice called from inside: "Gwendolyn? The pastor here."

She turned away from Lenwell, back toward the house full of mourners and memories. Back to where her father needed her to be the daughter her mother had raised, not the girl who'd lost more than innocence last night.

The radio played in someone's kitchen nearby, the familiar voice reading out the morning death announcements. Soon her mother's name would join that daily roll call of loss, another piece of proof that this wasn't just a terrible dream.

Her father's hand found hers as they sat to speak with the pastor. His fingers shook slightly, but his voice stayed smooth and sure as he discussed arrangements, hymns, all the details that needed attention. She held onto his strength like a lifeline, wondering how he managed to keep going when everything inside her wanted to shatter.

The day stretched ahead, full of decisions and visitors and moments that would blur together in memory. But somewhere out there, Lenwell waited, carrying half of her heart while the other half lay broken in this house of mourning. She didn't know how to hold all these pieces together - daughter, lover, grieving child, young woman - but she would have to find a way.

Her mother's empty chair watched from its corner, still holding the shape of absent presence. On the counter, Sister Jenkins' bread cooled beside Miss Mary's casserole, the scents mixing with coffee and sympathy, creating the familiar aroma of Caribbean mourning. Life would go on, different but continuing, carrying them all forward whether they were ready or not.

24

Another morning, Gwen woke to the sound of the radio in the kitchen. For one moment, everything felt normal - her father getting ready for factory work, the familiar voice reading out community announcements, the smell of someone's breakfast cooking next door.

Then memory crashed back, stealing her breath.

She lay still, unable to face a world where her mother no longer existed. The radio droned on - birthday greetings, community meetings, church events. Then the voice shifted tone, that slight change that marked the start of the death announcements.

Her father's footsteps stopped moving in the kitchen. The sound of his coffee cup settling in its saucer. Every morning they'd listened to these announcements, her mother always saying a prayer for each family named. N ow...

"It is with deep regret that we announce the death of Martha Richards, age 42, of Lodge Village..."

The words slammed into her chest like physical blows.

"...beloved wife of Denzil Richards and mother of Gw endolyn..."

A sound escaped her throat - not quite a cry, not quite a scream. Her father's footsteps moved fast toward her room, but she couldn't stop listening.

"...funeral arrangements will be announced later. May her soul rest in peace."

Her father's arms found her as she crumpled, holding her while those words echoed in her head. Beloved wife. Mother of Gwendolyn. Her name on the radio, connected forever to this loss, making it real in a way even last night's tears hadn't managed.

They sat together on her bed while the radio contin- ued its morning routine - more announcements, music, weather reports. Normal sounds that had no right to exist in this new, broken world.

"They going read it again tomorrow," her father said finally, his smooth voice rougher than she'd ever heard it. "And the next day. Three days they do that."

Three days of hearing her mother's death announced to the whole island. Three days of her own name linked to this loss. Three days of everyone knowing, everyone listening, everyone marking their family's pain in the rhythm of morning radio.

Her father's hand smoothed her hair, the same way her mother used to. "You want me stay home today?"

She shook her head against his shoulder. They needed normal things now - his factory work, the routine of days continuing. Even if nothing would ever be normal again.

When he left, she stayed in her room, listening to the house's empty spaces. The radio played on in the kitchen, volume turned low now, but she couldn't bring herself to turn it off. Her mother's voice lived in her memory, saying grace over breakfast, humming along to morning hymns, commenting on each death announced like she knew every family on the island.

Now their family's name would be on other people's lips, other mothers saying prayers for them, other families shaking their heads at the news of Martha Richards, age

42, beloved wife, mother of Gwendolyn, gone too soon from this world that kept turning despite everything.

132

25

The knocking started before the radio finished its morning program. Miss Mary first, then Miss Julie, then faces Gwen only half-recognized - women from church, neighbors she'd seen but never spoken to, all arriving with purpose in their steps and knowing looks in their eyes.

They moved through the house like a quiet tide, taking over spaces that still held her mother's last touches. The cup of half-finished tea her mother would never finish. The laundry basket of clothes she'd meant to iron. The shopping list on the counter with items they'd never buy.

"Go change out that nightdress," Miss Mary said, gentle but firm. "People go be coming all day."

The thought of facing people, of hearing their sympathy, made Gwen's stomach twist. But already she heard more voices in the yard, the murmur of concerned neighbors gathering in the morning light.

Her school uniform hung neat on its hook - her mother's last ironing. The sight of it broke something fresh inside her. She reached out to touch the crisp fabric, remembering how just yesterday morning she'd been worried about Geography homework and stolen moments with Lenwell. Now those concerns felt like they belonged to someone else, someone who still had a mother.

Miss Julie appeared with a cup of bush tea and a plate of warm raisin rolls. "Me just bake these," she said, setting them down. "You mother always love them with she morning tea."

The familiar sweet scent caught in Gwen's throat. How many mornings had she watched her mother eat these same rolls, brushing raisins from her fingers before heading to work? Now Miss Julie stood in their kitchen, bringing comfort food to a house that would never again know her mother's cooking.

More people arrived through the morning. The Mohammed family from next door brought food without pork. Sister Jenkins arrived with three different kinds of bread and her famous coconut tarts that Gwen's mother always praised at church gatherings. Each person carried something - food, prayers, memories of Martha Richards who'd always had a kind word and helping hand.

Through the front window, Gwen caught glimpses of Lenwell standing at the gate. He'd changed into his school uniform but made no move to leave for classes. Just stood there, uncertain, shifting from foot to foot like he wanted to come in but couldn't find the courage.

The sight of him sent guilt crashing through her chest. While he'd been touching her, kissing her, making her feel things she'd never felt before, her mother had been dying in a hospital bed. While she'd been lost in passion and discovery, her mother had been taking her last breaths. How could she face him now, knowing what they'd done in those precious final hours?

"That boy been standing there long time," Miss Mary said, following her gaze. "He look like he want come pay respect."

Gwen turned away from the window. "A can't..." The words caught in her throat.

Miss Mary's hand was gentle on her shoulder. "Whatever weighing on you mind, child, it no worth carrying alone."

But how could she explain? How could anyone understand the tangle of guilt and grief and shame that knotted her stomach every time she thought about that night? About choosing that moment for something that could have waited, should have waited.

The day stretched endless, filled with more visitors, more food, more sympathy. Women moved through their kitchen with practiced efficiency, storing casseroles in the fridge, arranging coconut tarts and raisin rolls on plates, speaking in low voices about arrangements and family to contact. Gwen wondered how long their house was going to be filled. When were they going to stop?

The factory called - her father could take as much time as he needed. The school sent word through one of the teachers who lived nearby - take the week, take longer, no rush. The phone rang constantly with people hearing the announcement, calling to confirm what they didn't want to believe.

Sharon came after school, still in her uniform, looking uncomfortable in the house full of mourners. She found

Gwen in the back garden, hiding from another wave of visitors.

"He stand by the gate all morning," she said softly. "Never even go to class. Just stand there hoping to see you."

The guilt rose fresh and sharp. "A can't see him right now."

"Girl, you act like you rob bank or something." Sharon's voice held more concern than judgment. "Whatever happen that night, it no change that you losing you mudda now. He just want be there for you."

But it did change things. Every time she thought about Lenwell, about his hands and his lips and the way he'd made her feel, the memory tangled with knowing her mother died while she was lost in those feelings. How could she ever separate the two now?

Her father came home early, looking lost in his own house again filled with people. She watched him accept hugs and handshakes, his smooth voice cracking only once when someone mentioned her mother's famous goat water - that rich, slow-simmered stew of goat meat and spices, thick with breadfruit and memories, the kind of dish that could bring a whole village to the table.

Night fell slow, taking the visitors with it. But their presence lingered in covered dishes filling the fridge, in the too-clean floors, in the rearranged furniture that made familiar rooms feel strange. The house felt both too empty and too full - empty of the one person they needed, full of everyone else's grief for her.

In her room, Gwen found her mother's scarf tucked into her school bag - put there days ago when the morning had been cool. The fabric still held her scent, that mixture of Pond's cream and coconut oil that meant safety and love and home. She pressed it to her face and finally let herself cry for everything lost in a single night - not just her mother, but also the simple peace of a world where love didn't come tangled with guilt, where joy didn't walk hand in hand with grief, where she could look at Lenwell without seeing all the ways she'd failed her mother in those final hours.

26

Her father didn't argue when she said she wanted to go back to school. They both knew staying home wouldn't change anything. Still, his hands shook slightly as he made her tea that morning, the way her mother used to.

Her spare uniform hung pressed on the back of her bedroom door - her father had tried his best with the iron, but the pleats didn't hold that crisp edge her mother always managed. She touched the fabric briefly, remembering how just days ago her biggest worry had been keeping it neat for school.

Sharon waited at their usual corner, but didn't speak as they walked. The morning air hung heavy with heat already, promising another blistering day. Market women set up their stalls, averting their eyes or calling out soft "morning" greetings as the girls passed. Everyone knew now - the death announcements had made sure of that.

The school yard fell quiet as they entered. Conversations stopped mid-sentence, eyes followed their progress across the packed dirt, whispers started up in their wake. Gwen kept her chin up, the way her mother had taught her. "No matter what people say or do, you hold you head high."

Their classroom felt different. Her classmates didn't know how to act, some murmuring awkward "sorry for you loss," others pretending nothing had changed. She felt Lenwell's presence like a physical thing - three rows back, one seat over. She didn't turn to look, but she knew he watched her, could feel the weight of his concern.

Teachers moved through their lessons carefully, speaking softer than usual, not calling on her even when her hand rose out of habit. Geography especially - her mother's favorite subject to hear about - felt wrong without her waiting at home to ask what they'd learned.

"You want go pink house?" Sharon asked when lunch break came. Then quickly: "Or me mudda pack extra."

But Gwen couldn't face the pink house now, couldn't walk those familiar paths knowing Lenwell might try to talk to her. "Not hungry."

They sat in their classroom instead, Sharon sharing the bread her mother had sent, though food tasted like ash in Gwen's mouth. Through it all, she felt Lenwell's eyes on her, knew he wanted to come over, to say something, to try to comfort her. But how could she accept comfort from the same hands that had touched her while her mother died?

Girls from other classes stopped by their desk during break, offering condolences like practiced adults. "She in a better place now," they said, and "God know best," and all the other things people said when they didn't know what to say.

"You want we go somewhere quiet?" Sharon asked as more people approached.

They ended up behind the classroom block where students usually snuck cigarettes, though no one smoked there now. The bread still held the warmth of morning baking, reminding Gwen of breakfasts her mother would never cook again.

"He want talk to you," Sharon said finally, breaking their silence. "Me see how he looking at you all morning."

"Me can't..." Gwen stopped, swallowed hard. "Every time me think bout him, bout that night..."

"You can't blame yourself for living just because she died."

But she did. Every breath, every heartbeat, every moment she'd spent in pleasure while her mother struggled for air - it all sat heavy as lead in her chest.

The afternoon classes passed in a blur. She copied notes without reading them, answered questions without hearing them, moved through the motions of normal life while feeling anything but normal. All the while, she kept her eyes forward, never turning to where she knew Lenwell sat, his presence burning like sunshine at her back.

When final bell rang, she hurried out before he could catch her, before she had to face those eyes that had looked at her with such tenderness that night. Sharon kept pace, understanding without words.

"He love you," she said softly as they walked home. "That no stop just because..."

"Don't." Gwen's voice broke on the word. "Please."

Her father waited at home, factory clothes still on, looking uncertain in their kitchen. "You want help with homework?" he asked, trying to fill spaces he'd never had to fill before.

She shook her head, retreating to her room where everything still held echoes of that morning her mother went to hospital. Books sat stacked on her desk, waiting for a focus she couldn't find.

Through her window, she watched the sun sink toward evening. Somewhere in Christ Church, Lenwell probably sat thinking of her, wanting to help, not understanding why she couldn't let him. But how could she separate the joy of first love from the pain of final loss when they'd happened in the same breath?

The radio played from someone's yard - not death announcements now, but the evening news program her mother always listened to while cooking. Regular life continued around them, as permanent as the sea meeting the shore, as unstoppable as time itself. But in her room, Gwen sat with her guilt and her grief, wondering if there would ever be a day when she could look at Lenwell without remembering everything else about that night.

27

The second death announcement hit harder than the first. Gwen stood in the kitchen, frozen by the familiar words washing over her: "Martha Richards, age 42, of Lodge Village..." Her father's hand found hers across the breakfast table, both of them listening as the radio spread their loss across the island once again.

More relatives had started arriving - aunts from town, cousins from the country, each bringing their own style of grief to crowd their small house. Aunt Shirley from Sandy Point took over the kitchen, tutting about how thin Denzil was getting. Uncle James from Basseterre spent hours in the front room telling stories about when her mother was young.

"You mother first time she cook," Aunt Shirley said, rolling out dough for dumplings, "she burn everything so bad we had to throw away the pot." She laughed, then caught herself, like joy wasn't allowed in a house of mourning.

School offered escape from the heaviness at home, but brought its own kind of weight. Lenwell had started leaving notes on her desk before she arrived each morning. Small things - "Me here if you need me" and "You no got to talk, just know me thinking bout you." She crumpled each one without reading them fully, but couldn't bring herself to throw them away.

"He trying," Sharon said during break time, watching Gwen add another crumpled note to her pocket. "That more than most boy would do."

But that was the problem. Lenwell wasn't like most boys. If he had been, maybe she could dismiss him, could pack away that night with all the other things she tried not to think about. Instead, his quiet persistence, his careful distance even while letting her know he cared - it made everything harder.

The geography teacher returned their tests from the week before. Her mother had helped her study for this one, quizzing her about river systems while cooking dinner. The B+ at the top of the page felt like both triumph and tragedy - her mother would never know she'd done well.

"You smart like she," her father said that evening when she showed him, his voice catching slightly. "She always know you was goin' be somebody."

More casseroles appeared on their doorstep, more sympathy cards, more visitors who clicked their tongues at how much she looked like her mother. The house filled with the sounds of people trying to help - Aunt Shirley singing hymns while cooking, Uncle James's deep laugh when sharing memories, cousins running in and out carrying messages and food.

But nothing could fill the spaces her mother left - the silence in the morning when no one called her to breakfast, the empty chair at the kitchen table, the unfinished shopping list still stuck to the fridge with her mother's last notes about what they needed.

Sharon stuck close at school, running interference when people's sympathy became too much. But she couldn't block everything. During lunch, Gwen overheard two girls from the form below:

"Them say she was with boy that night-"

"While she mother dying?"

"Girl, you no hear? That Lenwell boy-"

Sharon's sharp "Shut you mout'" cut them off, but the damage was done. Heat flooded Gwen's face as she hurried from the classroom, Sharon close behind.

"Them just talking foolishness," Sharon said once they found a quiet spot. "Nobody no know nothing."

But people did know, or at least suspected. She saw it in the way some teachers looked at her now, in the whispers that followed her through corridors, in how some girls switched from sympathy to judgment overnight.

That afternoon, she found Lenwell waiting by the mango tree where their paths usually crossed. She tried to hurry past, but his voice stopped her.

"Gwen." Just her name, soft and full of everything he couldn't say.

She kept walking, Sharon's hand firm on her arm, but his next words followed her: "Me no care what people say. Me just want..."

That night, alone in her room, she pulled out all his crumpled notes. Smoothed each one carefully on her desk, reading the words she'd been avoiding. His handwriting filled the pieces of paper like his presence filled the spaces in her mind - impossible to ignore, impossible to accept.

The radio still played from someone's yard, the evening news now instead of death announcements. Tomorrow they'd read her mother's name again, one last time. Tomorrow more relatives would arrive to help with funeral preparations. Tomorrow she'd have to face Lenwell across the classroom again, carrying the weight of what they'd shared and what they'd lost.

But tonight she sat with his notes spread before her, wondering how something could feel so right and so wrong at the same time. Outside her window, the mango tree that had witnessed so many of their secret moments swayed in the evening breeze, its leaves whispering things she wasn't ready to hear.

28

The final death announcement played like judgment. Gwen sat at breakfast, pushing food around her plate while the radio voice sealed her mother's passing into island memory. Her father's fork scraped against his plate - the only other sound in their crowded kitchen as aunts and cousins paused in their morning bustle to listen.

"Funeral on Saturday," Aunt Shirley announced. "Pastor coming later to plan service."

More relatives had arrived overnight - second cousins from Nevis, an uncle she barely remembered from St. Thomas. The house groaned under the weight of all their grief, all their good intentions. Every surface held some-

thing brought by caring hands - dishes that needed returning, sympathy cards, lists of people to call.

"You going school today?" her father asked, his voice
careful. "Could stay help with arrangements if you want."

She shook her head. School meant structure, meant
something normal in days that felt anything but. Even
facing Lenwell seemed better than sitting there listening to
relatives parse out the details of her mother's life and death.

Sharon waited at their corner, a brown paper bag in her
hand. "Me mudda send breakfast," she said, though they
both knew Gwen wasn't going to eat it.

The school yard chatter died as they approached. News
of Saturday's funeral had spread - she saw it in the way people watched her, in their whispered conversations. Even
teachers spoke softer, gentler, like she might break.

Lenwell's seat stayed empty that morning.

"He gone town with he fadda," Sharon whispered during break time. "Something bout suit for funeral."

The word hung between them - funeral. Final. Forever.
Gwen's chest tightened until she could hardly breathe.

"You want-"

"No." She cut Sharon off. "Me no want talk bout it."

But she couldn't escape it. After school, she walked into a house full of funeral plans. The pastor sat with her father at the kitchen table, discussing hymns and readings. Aunt Shirley and Uncle James argued about which cousins should be pallbearers. Someone had brought her mother's favorite dress for burial - it hung like a ghost in the front room.

Her father's voice carried from the kitchen: "She used to sing that one... when Gwen was small..."

She fled to her room, but even there she couldn't escape. The sound of her mother's favorite hymn drifted through her door - some ladies practicing in the kitchen. They'd sing it again on Saturday, when they put her mother in the ground.

A soft knock at her door. "Gwen?" Sharon's voice. "You fadda say you no come out for dinner..."

"Me no hungry."

The door opened anyway. Sharon carried a plate and something else - a folded piece of paper.

"He bring this just now," she said, setting both on Gwen's desk. "Say he sorry he no come school today, but he had to..."

Gwen turned away, but not before seeing her name in Lenwell's familiar handwriting. "Tek it back."

"No. He standing in de rain to bring this. Least you could do is read it."

Rain? She looked out her window. When had it started raining? How long had she been sitting there, lost in thoughts of Saturday?

After Sharon left, the note seemed to grow larger, more demanding. Finally, she unfolded it with shaking hands.

"Me know you no want see me," he'd written. "But me go be there Saturday. Not for people to talk, not for nothing but you need people who love you right now. Even if you no want me close, me go be there. Just so you know you no alone."

The words blurred as tears fell. Outside, the rain continued, washing away the day's heat. Outside of her room, her father's voice mixed with the pastor's, planning the service that would make everything final. Somewhere in the darkness, Lenwell was probably home now, maybe thinking of her, maybe regretting getting mixed up with a girl who couldn't separate love from loss.

Her mother's dress hung in the front room, waiting for Saturday. Everything waited for Saturday. But for now,

Gwen sat with Lenwell's note in her hands, wondering how he could still find the right words when she couldn't find any at all.

29

The day before her mother's funeral transformed their yard into something unrecognizable. Men from church arrived early, raising the huge white tent that would shelter mourners from sun or rain. The sound of hammers and voices mixed with the scent of fresh bread baking in every neighbor's kitchen - everyone preparing food for tomorrow's gathering.

Inside, the house hummed with activity. Aunt Shirley directed an army of cousins moving furniture, clearing space for the crowds they expected. Their front room had become a storage space for covered dishes arriving hourly - peas and rice, fresh baked bread, coconut tarts, salt fish cakes, all the tastes of comfort brought by knowing hands.

"They setting up chairs outside too," Sharon said, helping Gwen press her black dress for tomorrow. "Me see more truck coming with tents for de yard."

The iron moved smoothly over dark fabric while outside, other irons hissed against other black clothes - everyone preparing their mourning dress. The whole island, it seemed, would appear tomorrow to say goodbye.

Morning arrived too soon. Gwen stood in her room, the black dress feeling foreign against her skin, while outside car doors slammed and voices murmured. More people arriving, more sympathy to face.

Her father appeared in her doorway, straight and proper in his dark suit. For a moment, she saw her mother's absence like a physical thing between them - all the times she would have adjusted his tie, smoothed his collar, fussed over them both.

"Time," was all he said, his smooth voice rougher than usual.

The church filled beyond capacity, people standing in the back and spilling out the doors. Teachers sat together in pressed clothes and serious faces. Market women who'd known her mother all her life dabbed at eyes with handkerchiefs. Even Mr. Pemberton came, his usual excitement about geography replaced by quiet dignity.

Then she saw him.

Lenwell stood with his family, transformed by his dark suit into someone both familiar and strange. The jacket emphasized his broad shoulders, the crisp white shirt making his skin glow warm as roasted almond. He'd gotten his hair cut fresh - the low fade sharp and clean, making him look older, more mature. When he turned, their eyes met across the crowded church, and something caught in her chest - guilt and want and grief all tangled together.

"He look proper," Sharon whispered beside her, then fell silent at Gwen's sharp look.

But he did. The boy from their classroom, from sugar cane fields and stolen moments, had become something else in that suit. A man, almost. Someone solid and sure, even as his eyes held all the uncertainty of watching her carry this weight he couldn't help with.

Her father noticed too. After the service, as people filed past with murmured condolences, Lenwell approached with his parents. His father spoke proper words about loss and sympathy, but Lenwell just stood straight and respectful, his eyes never leaving Gwen's face.

"You coming to the house?" Her father's voice carried that smooth quality, but something else too - recognition maybe, of what it meant for a young man to show such respect.

"Yes sir," Lenwell's voice came quiet but firm. "If that alright."

"Come." Just that one word, but it shifted something between them all.

The drive home felt endless. More cars than their small street had ever seen lined both sides, people walking in their Sunday best toward the white tent that transformed their yard into a gathering place. The scent of food filled the air - chicken cook up mixing with bread pudding, coconut tarts warming in the afternoon sun, ginger beer and sorrel being poured into glasses.

Inside, women moved with practiced efficiency, setting out food on every surface. Outside, men arranged chairs in the shade, discussing weather and crops and anything but the reason they gathered. Children darted between adults, shushed quickly if their play grew too loud.

Lenwell stayed proper, helping carry chairs, fetching drinks for older folks, everything a young man should do at a funeral gathering. But Gwen felt his presence like heat from a flame - wanting to move closer even while knowing she should stay away.

"You mudda would be proud," Miss Mary said, watching Gwen accept condolences with quiet grace. "She raise you right."

But what would her mother think of how her heart jumped every time Lenwell passed nearby? What would she say about the way guilt and attraction fought in Gwen's chest every time she caught sight of him in that suit, looking like every dream she shouldn't be having at her mother's funeral?

The afternoon stretched long, sun beating down on the white tent while people came and went. Stories about her mother filled the air - tales of her kindness, her cooking, her way of helping anyone who needed it. Each memory felt like a stone added to the weight in Gwen's chest, a reminder of everything they'd lost.

Sharon stayed close, running interference when grief threatened to overwhelm, bringing cold drinks when the heat pressed too hard. But she couldn't block everything. Couldn't stop Gwen from seeing how Lenwell watched her from across the tent, couldn't prevent the moment their hands brushed as he passed her a glass of ginger beer, couldn't erase the electricity that still sparked between them even on this most solemn of days.

Evening brought cooler air but no relief. More food appeared - fish cakes and johnny cakes for those still gathered, sweet bread and strong tea for those who'd stay late. Through it all, Gwen moved like a ghost in her black dress, accepting sympathy, thanking people for coming, trying not to notice how Lenwell's white shirt glowed in the falling dark like a beacon she couldn't help but see.

30

The Monday after the funeral, their house felt hollow. The tent was gone, leaving bare patches in their yard where grass had died under heavy feet. Inside, borrowed chairs had been returned, but empty spaces remained where furniture had been moved, like missing teeth in a familiar smile.

Her father stood at the stove that morning, attempting to make breakfast. The eggs came out hard as rocks, but Gwen ate them anyway, watching him try to fill roles that had always been her mother's.

"Me could learn," he said, scraping burnt edges from the pan. "You mudda start somewhere too."

School waited, unchanged by their loss. The same walls, same desks, same faces - though people looked at her different now. The girl who'd lost her mother. The girl who wore black ribbons in her hair. The girl who...

Lenwell sat three rows back, one seat over, just like always. But something had shifted since the funeral. Since her father's quiet "come" and his proper behavior under the white tent. Since she'd seen him in that suit, looking like someone who could carry the weight of hard things.

"He still watching you," Sharon whispered during break time.

Gwen nodded, not trusting her voice. The guilt still sat in her chest, but different now - not as sharp, not as consuming. Like a wound starting to heal, tender but no longer bleeding.

Their classroom felt emptier without the constant stream of sympathy that had filled it before the funeral. Teachers had stopped being so careful around her, letting normal routine return. Even Mr. Pemberton's enthusiasm for river systems crept back into his voice.

At lunch break, she found herself looking toward the pink house. She hadn't gone there since before - hadn't wanted food or company or anything but the comfort of grief. But today...

"You want go?" Sharon asked, following her gaze.

"Maybe tomorrow."

But they both heard what she really meant. Maybe soon. Maybe things could start being normal again, even if normal looked different now.

Her father tried cooking again that evening. The chicken came out dry, the rice too soft, but he didn't give up. "You mudda burn plenty pot before she learn," he said, his smooth voice holding something like hope. "We go figure this out."

Through her window that night, she watched stars appear one by one. Somewhere across the dark stretch of villages between them, Lenwell probably looked at the same stars. The thought didn't bring the usual stab of guilt. Instead, she felt something else - a quiet acknowledgment that love and loss could exist in the same heart without breaking it.

Her mother's scarf still hung on her bedpost, the scent of Pond's cream and coconut oil fading a little more each day. But maybe that was how it worked - grief changing shape, guilt losing its edge, life finding ways to continue even when you thought it couldn't.

Tomorrow would come, bringing with it all the small challenges of living without her mother. But tonight, Gwen lay in her bed listening to her father humming in the kitchen - off-key but trying - and thought about suits and stars and the possibility that some things could heal without being forgotten.

31

"You better come eat before it spoil," her father called from the kitchen. Two weeks of practice had improved his cooking - at least now the rice didn't stick to the bottom of the pot. Every morning he tried something new, determined to master their old routines in his own way.

At school, life had settled into new patterns. Sharon still walked with her every morning, but they'd started stopping at the pink house again for lunch. The first time felt strange - like betraying her grief by wanting normal things. But hunger eventually won over guilt.

She hadn't spoken to Lenwell since the funeral, but she'd stopped avoiding his eyes across the classroom.

Sometimes she caught him watching her, that same careful concern in his face, but he kept his distance. No more notes, no more messages through Sharon. Just quiet presence, like he understood she needed space to figure out who she was now.

"Look like rain coming," Sharon said as they left school that afternoon. Dark clouds gathered over the mountains, bringing that sharp pre-rain smell that meant serious weather approaching.

They hurried past the sugar cane fields where young stalks bent in the strengthening wind. The cane had grown tall since planting season, green blades whispering secrets to each other as the storm wind moved through them. Lightning flickered in the distance, followed by the low growl of thunder rolling across the fields.

The first heavy drops fell just as they reached Sharon's house. "You sure you no want wait it out?"

But Gwen shook her head. Sometimes rain felt good - like it could wash away things that needed washing. The sugar cane fields looked different in the rain, the tall stalks shimmering silver-green as water ran down their blades, making them dance in the wind.

She was soaked by the time she reached their gate. Through the curtain of rain, she saw her father's Bug in the driveway, home early from the factory. Strange - he never came home before dark these days.

The front door stood open to catch the rain breeze. Her father sat alone at the kitchen table, staring at something she couldn't see. He looked up when she entered, water dripping from her uniform.

"Go change," he said, that smooth voice holding something she couldn't read. "Then come back. We got to talk."

In her room, she peeled off her wet clothes, mind racing. Her father's face had held that same expression he'd worn the morning they took her mother to hospital - like he had news he didn't want to give.

"Sit down," he said when she returned. He hadn't moved from his spot at the table. "Me got something me need tell you."

His shoulders looked heavier than usual, like they carried more than factory tiredness. He stared at his hands for a long moment before speaking.

"You got aunt in Orlando."

"What?"

"Me sister Laurel. She move up there long time before you born."

Gwen gripped the edge of the table. In all her life, she'd never heard of an Aunt Laurel, never known her father had a sister in America. "How come you never say nothing bout she before?"

His fingers drummed against the table, a nervous movement she'd never seen from him. "We ain't been close, me and Laurel. But she hear bout you mudda.." He stopped, swallowed hard. "She say she could take you."

The words hung in the air between them, heavy as lead. "Take me?"

"To Orlando. Give you chance for proper education. Better life than what this island could give."

"But..." Her voice caught. "Me no want go nowhere. Me got school here, me got Sharon, me got-" She stopped before saying Lenwell's name, but her father's eyes flickered like he heard it anyway.

"Man can't raise woman child right," he said, that smooth voice rougher now. "Some things only a mudda could teach. My mudda used to say fowl can't teach duck to swim."

"We managing fine," she protested. "You learning to cook, me learning to-"

"Managing ain't enough." He pushed back from the table. "You mudda want more for you than just managing. Than just surviving. She want you spread you wings, fly higher than this place could let you."

"You never even tell me bout this sister before today. Now you want send me live with she?"

"Laurel different now. She marry good, got proper house, everything set up nice nice." He wouldn't meet her eyes. "She know how raise young lady right. Know things fadda can't teach."

Gwen thought about Sharon, about their walks to school, about pink house lunches and shared secrets. About Lenwell's careful distance since the funeral, like he knew she needed space to heal. About all the pieces of her life here that were finally starting to feel normal again.

"But..." Tears choked her words. "What about we two? We supposed to stick together now."

Her father's hands shook slightly as they found hers across the table. "Sometimes love mean doing the hard thing. You mudda know that. Why you think she and me been planning this long time?"

"You and she what?"

"Been talking bout it since she first get sick. She make me promise - if anything happen, me wouldn't let you settle for small life here."

The betrayal hit fresh - not just her father making this decision, but her mother planning it too. All those hospital visits, all those quiet conversations she couldn't hear, had been about sending her away.

"Orlando just like what you see on them TV show you does watch," he said, trying to soften the blow. "Proper high school with lockers and everything."

But she didn't want Bayside High. Didn't want Lisa Turtle's perfect American life. She wanted her mother back. Wanted her father to fight harder to keep them together. Wanted...

"Me no going." She stood so fast her chair scraped against the floor. "You can't make me."

"Gwendolyn." Just her name, but weighted with everything he couldn't say. "Please. Me trying do right by you mudda. By you."

"If you trying do right, let me stay." The tears came hot now. "We could make it work, just us two."

He shook his head, and in that movement she saw how final this was. How decisions had been made long before this conversation, shaped by island wisdom about fathers and daughters, by her mother's dreams for her future, by love that sometimes looked like letting go.

"Ticket already book," he said quietly. "Laurel expecting you before school start."

Outside, rain still fell, running down the windows like tears. She could see the sugar cane fields in the distance, bending but not breaking in the storm wind, somehow staying rooted even as everything around them changed. But she couldn't be like them. Couldn't stay rooted in this place that held everything she loved.

She fled to her room, leaving him at the kitchen table. Through her window, the familiar sight of Lodge blurred through rain and tears - the houses where families stayed whole, the paths she walked with Sharon, the fields where she'd first tasted love with Lenwell. All of it about to become memory, traded for a strange new world she'd only seen through a TV screen.

Her father's footsteps moved through the kitchen outside her room, heavy with the weight of his decision. She heard something clatter in the sink, then a sound she'd never heard before - a sob, quickly muffled, like he was trying to be strong even when no one could see.

32

Sharon waited at their corner the next morning, already talking about some drama with her little brother. She stopped mid-sentence when she saw Gwen's face.

"What happen?"

Gwen couldn't say it yet. Not here on the street where anybody could hear, where she'd have to say the words out loud and make them real. They walked in silence past the sugar cane fields, past the market women setting up their stalls, past all the familiar pieces of her life that would soon become memory.

Finally, in the quiet space behind their classroom before other students arrived: "Me fadda sending me Orlando."

"What?" Sharon grabbed her arm. "America Orlando?"

Gwen nodded, tears threatening again. "He got sister there. Aunt me never even hear bout before."

"When?"

"Before school start. American school."

Sharon's face did something complicated - excitement warring with devastation. Everyone knew America meant opportunity, meant something bigger than island life could offer. But everyone also knew what it meant to be left behind.

"Girl..." Sharon's voice caught. Then, trying for lightness: "You go be living Save by the Bell for true."

"Me no want live no TV show." The tears came then, hot and unstoppable. "Me want stay here with you, with..."

She couldn't say his name, but Sharon understood. They both looked across the slowly filling classroom to where Lenwell sat with his friends, not yet noticing their quiet drama in the corner.

"How you go tell him?"

"Me no know if me should." Gwen wiped her eyes with her sleeve. "Maybe better if he just..."

"No." Sharon's voice turned firm. "You can't just disappear on him like that. Not after everything."

Everything. That night when her mother died. The funeral in his proper suit. All the careful distance he'd kept since then, respecting her grief while letting her know he still cared. How could she tell him she was leaving just when things might have started healing between them?

The day passed in a blur. Teachers' voices washed over her while she looked at everything through new eyes - the familiar walls she'd never see again, the faces she'd grown up with, the life she was about to leave behind.

At home, her father had already started sorting through her things. "Laurel say she got proper room set up for you," he said, holding up her old school books. "But we got to decide what worth shipping and what you could just get new there."

She fled to her room, unable to watch him dismantle her life piece by piece. But even there, everything looked different now. The posters on her walls that wouldn't survive the journey. The pile of novels Sharon had lent her that would need returning. The ribbon from the funeral that still hung on her mirror, black silk fading to grey.

"You know," Sharon said at lunch the next day, "them got proper mall in Orlando. Big big mall with escalator and everything."

"Like in Bayside?"

"Better. Me cousin send picture from when she visit she aunt there. Everything shiny shiny."

But Gwen didn't want shiny American things. She wanted pink house lunches and sugar cane field shortcuts and the weight of island history in every stone wall they passed. She wanted...

"He looking this way again," Sharon whispered.

Gwen didn't turn, couldn't face Lenwell's concerned gaze. How could she tell him that every time she caught him watching her now, it felt like goodbye?

That evening, going through her closet, she found the notes he'd left on her desk after her mother died - all the ones she'd crumpled but couldn't throw away. His neat handwriting blurred through fresh tears as she read them again. "Me here if you need me." But soon she wouldn't be here at all.

"Child?" Her father's voice carried from the kitchen. "You want try this stew me making? Think me nearly get it right this time."

She went to the kitchen, watching him stir the pot with the same careful concentration he brought to his factory work. Everything he did lately felt like love and apology mixed together - trying to be both mother and father while knowing he couldn't be either, not the way she needed.

"Laurel say she got good kitchen," he said, not looking up from his stirring. "Maybe she teach you proper cooking, way you mudda would have."

The words stuck in her throat: But I want you to teach me, even if you burn everything first. I want to stay and figure it out together. Instead she just nodded, tasting his too-salty stew and pretending it was perfect.

Later, she sat at her window watching lights come on across Lodge as evening settled. The sugar cane fields stretched dark toward Christ Church where Lenwell lived, where he was probably doing homework or helping his mother cook or living his normal life not knowing she would soon be gone. Sharon was right - she had to tell him. Had to find the words to explain how you could want to stay somewhere with your whole heart and still end up leaving.

Her mother's voice seemed to whisper from every corner of the room: Sometimes love mean doing the hard thing. But which was harder - staying or leaving? And how many different ways could a heart break before it couldn't heal anymore?

33

The morning sun barely touched the tops of the cane fields when Sharon appeared at their corner. They walked in silence past Miss Mary's yard where washing hung still and heavy in the airless morning.

"You go tell him?" Sharon asked finally.

Gwen shook her head, watching a market woman arrange her mangoes just so, each fruit placed carefully like how her own future was being arranged without her say.

"He got right to know, girl." Sharon's voice gentle but firm. "Especially after everything..."

Everything. The word caught in Gwen's chest like sharp cane leaf. After her mother. After the funeral. After all his careful distance while she carried her grief. Her feet slowed as they passed the bus stop where she'd seen him waiting that other morning, back when life held different possibilities.

She stopped sudden, making Sharon stumble. "Me going tell him today."

"You mean at lunch? Or after-"

"No." The word came fast, surprising them both. "Right now."

Sharon's eyes widened. After weeks of watching Gwen avoid Lenwell, of crumpled notes and careful distance, this felt like rain breaking drought. "What you want me say?"

Gwen's heart raced like it might burst free. "Tell him meet me by de bus stop. Like before."

"You sure?" Sharon studied her friend's face. "After all this time..."

"What me got to lose now?" The words came bitter as young cane. "Few more days and me gone anyway."

They reached the school gates where Lenwell stood with his friends, looking like any other morning except for how her chest tightened seeing him. Sharon squeezed her hand once before crossing the yard toward him, while Gwen waited by the corner, unable to watch, unable to look away.

When Sharon returned, her face held something between worry and hope. "He say yes. But he want know if you sure-sure."

The familiar routine felt strange now - him taking the first bus while she waited those seven minutes that seemed to stretch as endless as the road to Basseterre. She watched him slip away from his friends, saw how he glanced back once like he still couldn't believe she'd asked for this. Nobody else looked twice - why would they? But she saw the tension in his shoulders, the careful way he held himself, like he too remembered their last time together and everything that came after.

When her bus finally came, she climbed aboard with trembling hands, memories of that other morning making her stomach twist. Through the window, Christ Church looked strange, like seeing it through someone else's eyes - the mango trees heavy with almost-ripe fruit, clothes hanging still on lines between houses, guinea grass bending in the morning breeze.

Lenwell waited under the same breadfruit tree, but uncertainty filled every line of his body. His eyes searched her face, looking for answers to questions he hadn't asked yet. "You sure you want..."

She nodded, words stuck in her throat. His hand found hers slowly, carefully, like he feared she might pull away. Each step toward his house felt weighted with everything unsaid between them, with all the grief and guilt that had kept them apart.

The front step creaked under their feet, familiar and strange at once. Inside, the narrow hallway seemed longer, the walk to his room taking forever. That slight slope in his floor still caught her off guard, making her stumble slightly. His hand steadied her elbow, gentle like she might break.

His room looked different in morning light - the blue and white sheets almost too bright, the cricket trophies watching from their shelf, everything neat and certain like him. A breeze moved through his window, carrying the scent of someone's wood fire, the sound of children play- ing hooky down by the ghaute, a cock still crowing late into morning.

When he reached for her, his hands shook. "Gwen..." His voice held weeks of watching her from across class- rooms, of respecting her grief, of waiting. "If you no read y..."

But she moved closer, needing to forget everything except how he felt, how he smelled like clean clothes and young man and possibilities that were slipping away too fast. His shirt rough then smooth under her fingers, her uniform joining it on the sloping floor, each piece of clothing marking steps toward something that felt both familiar and new.

The blue and white sheets caught them like last time, but everything else felt different. His hands moved slower, more careful, like he remembered how grief could tangle with wanting. She traced her own patterns across his skin, trying to memorize everything - the strength in his arms, the smoothness of his chest, the way his breath caught when she touched him certain ways.

When they joined, the pleasure came sweeter than before but heavier too, weighted with everything that had happened since last time. She pressed her face against his neck, breathing in the scent of him, trying to hold onto this moment that felt like both healing and breaking.

After, with the sheet pulled over them both, the words she'd been holding spilled out: "Me fadda sending me away."

His whole body went still. "What you mean?"

"Orlando." Her voice barely a whisper. "He got sister there me never even know bout before. Want me finish school proper way."

"But..." His arms tightened around her like he could keep her there by strength alone. Then he sat up sudden, hope flaring in his eyes. "You could stay with we. Me mudda always saying she want another daughter-"

"Lenwell." His name came soft, sad. How could she explain that island life had rules? That no family could take in another's child without tongues wagging? That her father's heart would shatter if she chose someone else's home over his plans for her future?

"Then me go find way come too." His voice held that same sureness she remembered from the funeral, like wanting something bad enough could make it happen. "After school finish-"

"You know that no go work." The tears came then, hot against his chest. "You got you whole life here, you family..."

"You suppose to be me life." The words caught rough in his throat. But they both heard what he couldn't say - that young love, no matter how sweet, couldn't change the way their world worked. Couldn't stop fathers from making choices for their children, couldn't keep families together across oceans.

They lay quiet then, listening to life moving around them - children's voices carrying from the school they should be at, someone's donkey braying in a nearby field, a truck grinding gears as it climbed the hill toward town. Each sound marking minutes slipping away from them.

"When?" he asked finally, his fingers moving gentle through her hair.

"End of month." She pressed closer, trying to burn the memory of him into her skin. "Before American school start."

His hands traced paths over her shoulders, her back, her face - like he was making maps he could follow later in dreams. When he kissed her again, it held everything they couldn't say - about guilt and grief and love that came too late and would end too soon.

Morning grew older around them, marking time they couldn't stop. Soon they'd have to leave this room with its sloping floor and watching trophies, return to a world where people had plans for their futures that didn't include each other. But for now, they held on in the quiet they'd found together, where love felt as real as the sun breaking through morning clouds, as unstoppable as waves against the shore, as precious as the last sweet piece of cane shared between young hearts.

34

Lenwell walked her to the main road, both of them quiet with the weight of what had just happened, what she'd just told him. They stood under the almond tree where buses usually slowed, his hand still holding hers like he could keep her there if he just held on tight enough.

When the first bus appeared, its gears grinding as it rattled down the hill, she hesitated. Her fingers tightened around his, as if holding on for just a second longer might change something—might make the morning stop unfolding the way it was meant to.

The bus pulled up with a sigh of brakes, the driver pausing, waiting. She should have lifted her hand. Should have stepped forward. But she didn't.

His fingers brushed hers one last time, brief and desperate, before he stepped back, giving her space to go.

The driver lingered, then, seeing no movement, shut the doors and pulled away.

She swallowed hard, watching it disappear down the road. Another bus would come. And this time, she'd have to get on.

When the next one arrived, she stepped forward, her legs feeling heavier than they should. The bus driver, an older man with weary eyes, held out his hand, and she placed the fare into his palm, the coins cool against her fingers before he closed his fist around them. No one else was on board. Just her, the driver, and the quiet hum of the engine.

She moved to a seat near the window, the village shrinking behind her as the bus rumbled forward. The narrow roads, the pastel houses, the swaying cane fields—everything she'd known her whole life—faded bit by bit.

The ride felt endless. Her uniform, hastily straightened, still held wrinkles that spoke of things she couldn't hide. Her skin remembered every place Lenwell had touched, while her heart felt heavy with the truth she'd finally told him.

Miss Julie stood in her yard as Gwen walked the last stretch home, her sharp eyes taking in everything - the crushed uniform, the too-early hour for someone who should've been in school. "You alright, child?" But her tone said she already knew the answer.

Inside their house, evidence of her coming departure spread like morning shadows. A cardboard box from the grocery shop sat half-filled with books her father thought worth sending. Her mother's old suitcase - the good one with the strong handle - waited in the corner, already cleaned and ready.

"That you, Gwen?" Her father's voice carried from the kitchen. He wasn't supposed to be home yet.

She found him at the table, papers spread before him like gentle accusations. Plane tickets printed with her name. Forms for American school. A letter from Aunt Laurel with an address she'd have to learn to call home.

"Them want you school records," he said without looking up. "And something call immunization papers from clinic."

His hands moved careful through the documents, like each one was delicate as young sugar cane leaf. She watched him sort and organize, wondering how long he'd been planning this, how many quiet moments he'd spent making arrangements while she thought life might stay the same.

"Laurel say she already fix up you room." His smooth voice caught slightly. "Put new curtains and everything."

The smell of someone's cooking drifted through their window - rice and saltfish probably, the familiar scents making Gwen's chest tight. Soon she'd be somewhere with different foods, different spices, where people didn't know how to season pot like island women did.

"Me run into Sharon mudda at market," her father continued. "She say she got some clothes she think might fit you. Things proper for America weather."

America weather. Like it was a different kind of sun that shone there, a different kind of rain that fell. She thought about Lenwell's hands on her skin just hours ago, how they'd felt like home and heartbreak mixed together. How could she explain to her father that she was leaving more than just weather behind?

Her father gathered the papers carefully, tucking them into a folder she recognized - the same one that had held her mother's hospital documents. "You better go change before somebody see you uniform looking so." His eyes held knowing but no judgment. "And Gwendolyn? Next time you skip school, at least press you clothes proper after."

Heat flooded her face as she fled to her room. But his words followed, gentle as aloe on sunburn - not angry, just sad maybe, like he understood some things didn't need punishing because life would do that all on its own.

Her room felt smaller now, boxes claiming more space each day. Sharon had helped her start sorting yesterday - things to pack, things to give away, things that wouldn't survive the journey. Like that poster of Bob Marley her mother had pretended not to see. Like the pile of Lenwell's crumpled notes she couldn't bring herself to throw away.

The phone rang just as she finished changing. Sharon's voice came through worried: "You make it home alright? He alright?"

"Yeah." But they both heard what she wasn't saying.

"He no even come back to school. Devon say he just walk and walk, all round de football field like he looking for something he lose."

Looking for something he lose. The words echoed in her chest like stones dropped in deep water. Wasn't that what they were all doing now? Looking for pieces of a life that was slipping away faster than they could hold it?

Through her window, she watched shadows stretch longer across their yard. The mango tree that had seen so many of her secrets swayed gentle in the afternoon breeze, its leaves whispering things that sounded like goodbye.

35

Morning sun caught the dew on Miss Mary's bougainvillea as Gwen walked past, each drop holding a different color like tiny captured rainbows. Miss Mary stood at her gate, her eyes soft with knowing as she watched Gwen approach.

"You going away?" The old woman's voice came gentle as breeze through young cane. "You fadda tell me last night."

Gwen nodded, her throat too tight for words. The weight of Miss Mary's hand on her arm felt like blessing and burden both.

"Sometimes," Miss Mary said, "life take we places we no think we ready for. But you stronger than you know, child. Just like you mudda was."

The comparison stung sweet as green mango. Gwen hurried on, tears threatening, to where Sharon waited at their corner. Her friend's face held everything they couldn't say.

"Me mudda pack extra food today," Sharon said as they walked. "She say you too thin these days."

The familiar path to school felt precious now, every step marking memories she'd have to leave behind - the corner shop where they bought penny candy as children, the huge flamboyant tree that bloomed red as heart's blood every spring, the shortcut through the neighbor's yard where the old donkey used to graze.

In her classroom, Gwen's eyes kept drifting to the empty spaces between present and future. Her mother's old suitcase waited at home, cleaned and ready, alongside the new blue one her father had brought home - its wheels too smooth, its surface too bright, everything about it screaming foreign and different.

Mr. Pemberton's voice rose and fell at the front of the class, talking about earth's shifting plates, but Gwen barely heard him. Instead, she found herself memorizing smaller things - how morning light slanted through the wooden shutters, the way chalk dust caught in sunbeams, the slight creak of the floor under their desks.

At lunch break, they stayed in their classroom, sharing salt fish and johnny cake that Sharon's mother had wrapped careful in wax paper. Through the doorway, Lenwell stood like a shadow against sunlight, his eyes holding questions neither of them had answers for.

"You think things different there?" Gwen asked suddenly. "Like how people be?"

Sharon was quiet for a moment, considering. "Jennifer cousin say them got washing machine that talk to you. Tell you when you clothes done and everything."

"Me no want no talking washing machine." Gwen's voice caught. "Me just want..."

But she couldn't finish. What she wanted sat in their classroom doorway, stood in her father's kitchen trying to cook proper meals, lay buried in the cemetery where her mother rested. What she wanted wasn't something you could pack in any suitcase, no matter how new or bright.

That evening, she stood in her room between her two bags - her mother's old faithful brown one that had carried their lives so many times, and this new blue thing with its eager wheels. Everything about them felt like choices she hadn't made, paths already chosen for her.

The phone rang in the kitchen. Sharon's voice came through soft: "He by the mango tree."

Gwen's heart jumped. Through her window, Lenwell's shape stood dark against the evening sky, still as the mountains behind Lodge. How many nights had he stood there since she told him? How many more would he stand there after she was gone?

"You want me tell him something?" Sharon asked.

The tears came then, hot and unstoppable. What could she say? That she was sorry? That she wished things were different? That her heart felt like it was splitting open, spilling everything she loved across the distance between where she was and where she had to go?

"Just..." Her voice broke on the word. "Tell him me sorry."

Through her window, she watched Lenwell's shape blur in the gathering dark. The mango tree's leaves moved gentle in the evening breeze, whispering things that sounded like memories, like promises, like goodbyes that came too soon no matter how long you saw them coming.

36

Her last day of school came too soon. Gwen stood in front of her uniform hanging on the door - pressed sharp one final time, though soon it would hang empty like a ghost of everything she was leaving behind.

Her father had tried making proper breakfast, the eggs only slightly burnt this time. They ate in silence, the morning radio playing songs that felt sadder somehow, like even the music knew things were ending.

"You want me walk with you?" he asked, his smooth voice careful. But she shook her head. This last walk to school belonged to her and Sharon, to the friendship they'd built step by step since primary school days.

Sharon waited at their corner, her eyes already red. They didn't speak as they walked, both knowing any words would break the dam holding back their tears. The morning felt heavy with last things - last time passing the corner shop, last time cutting through the neighbor's yard, last time walking this path they'd traced a thousand times before.

The classroom hushed when they entered. Word had spread that this was her last day, that tomorrow she'd be on a plane heading toward a life none of them could quite imagine. Even Mr. Pemberton's voice held something different when he called her name for attendance one final time.

Lenwell sat in his usual spot, but today his eyes never left her. She felt his gaze like physical touch - memorizing, grieving, holding on to what little time remained. During break time, she caught him writing something, his pen moving urgent across paper like he had too much to say and not enough time to say it.

"Last time we go eat together," Sharon said at lunch, but her voice broke before she could finish. They sat under the mango tree in the school yard, sharing johnny cake and memories, neither mentioning how this same tree stood outside Gwen's window where Lenwell kept his evening vigil.

The final bell rang too soon and not soon enough. As students filed out, some stopped to hug her, others just nodded, everyone understanding that something was ending that couldn't be properly farewelled.

She lingered in the doorway, looking back at her empty desk. Tomorrow someone else would sit there, would look out that window, would live the life she was leaving behind. A movement caught her eye - Lenwell, placing something on her desk. When he straightened, their eyes met across the space between them.

"Gwen..." Just her name, but it held weeks of unsaid things.

She couldn't move, couldn't speak. His footsteps crossed the distance between them, slow but sure, like he'd been waiting for this moment.

"Me write you something," he said, his voice low. "For when you gone."

The folded paper felt warm from his hands. She tucked it in her pocket without reading, knowing she couldn't bear his words just yet, not here, not now.

"Me never go forget-" he started, but she pressed her fingers to his lips. Some things, once said, couldn't be taken back. Some goodbyes hurt less if they stayed partly unspoken.

Sharon waited outside, giving them this moment but staying close enough to catch Gwen when she needed catching. When Lenwell finally stepped back, his eyes bright with tears he wouldn't let fall, Sharon moved forward to link her arm through Gwen's.

They walked home the long way, past the cane fields where young stalks stretched toward sky, past the pink house where they'd shared so many lunches, past all the places that had shaped their friendship. At Gwen's gate, Sharon hugged her tight.

"Me coming early tomorrow," she said against Gwen's shoulder. "Before you leave."

Inside, her father sat at the kitchen table, airline tickets laid out neat beside her passport. Tomorrow morning her father's bug would carry her away from everything she knew, everything she loved. Her mother's old suitcase and the new blue one waited by the door, both packed full of things that somehow had to substitute for home.

In her room, she finally pulled out Lenwell's letter. His handwriting filled the page with memories - of sugar cane shared sweet between them, of moments stolen in morning light, of love that came too late and ended too soon. The last lines blurred as her tears fell:

"Some things no got proper goodbye. Some things just got to live in we heart until maybe one day..."

She pressed the letter to her chest, feeling her heart beat against the words he'd written. Outside her window, the mango tree stood empty against darkening sky. For the first time since she'd told him she was leaving, Lenwell wasn't there. Maybe some goodbyes were easier if you spread them over many nights instead of saving them all for one final moment.

Tomorrow would come too soon, would carry her toward a future she hadn't chosen. But tonight she held his words against her heart, letting them mix with her tears until she couldn't tell which was which, just knowing that both would follow her across whatever distance lay ahead.

Epilogue

Morning arrived, gray and quiet, as if even the sun hesitated to rise. Gwen stood at her window one last time, watching light creep across the yard where so many of her stories had played out. The mango tree's leaves hung still in the airless dawn, heavy with dew and memory.

Her father moved through the kitchen with careful steps, like any sudden noise might break something precious. The scent of lemongrass tea mixed with stewing saltfish - him trying to make her one last proper island breakfast. She watched him struggle with the onions, his cuts uneven, pieces too large, but she said nothing. Just sat at their table, memorizing how morning light caught his face as he concentrated on getting something right for her.

A knock at the back door - Sharon, early like she promised, eyes already swimming. She carried a small package wrapped in brown paper. "Me mudda make you favorite," she said, her voice threatening to crack. "For de plane."

The two bags waited by the front door, holding everything that could be packed, but not everything that meant home. How could sixteen years of life be measured in airline weight limits?

Through the window, dawn painted the sky in shades of goodbye. Movement by the mango tree caught her eye. Lenwell stood there in the growing light, still as the mountains behind Lodge, watching her house like he could keep her there by the strength of his gaze alone. Sharon squeezed her hand under the table.

"Me go tell him you coming out?" Sharon whispered.

Gwen nodded, her throat too tight for words. She watched through the window as Sharon crossed the yard, as Lenwell's shape became clearer in the morning light. He wore his uniform crisp and perfect like the suit from her mother's funeral, each pleat sharp enough to cut paper, like he wanted her last memory of him to be something beautiful and precise.

Her father disappeared into his room while she walked out to where Lenwell waited.

The path to him felt longer than it should have, each step weighted with everything she couldn't say. The morning air was thick, humming with the distant sounds of a world that hadn't stopped for them—roosters crowing, a neighbor's radio crackling to life, the rustle of wind through cane fields. But for her, for him, time had slowed, stretched thin like the space between them. She wanted to hold on to these last few steps, to delay the moment when goodbye would no longer be a possibility but a certainty.

Up close, she could see he hadn't slept, could see how his hands shook slightly as they reached for hers.

"Me just want..." he started, but the words caught. Instead, he pressed something into her palm—a piece of sugar cane, young and sweet, cut fresh this morning from someone's field. Their eyes met over this final gift, both remembering other pieces shared in secret places, other moments that had tasted just as sweet.

They stood quiet under the mango tree, holding each other while morning light grew stronger around them. Everything they needed to say passed without words - in the way his fingers traced her face like memorizing a map, in how her tears fell silent against his crisp uniform, in the gentle press of his lips against her forehead one last time.

When they finally pulled apart, Sharon waited a respectful distance away, giving them this moment before claiming her own goodbye. As Lenwell stepped back, his eyes bright with tears he wouldn't let fall, Sharon moved forward with arms already opening.

"You go write?" Sharon asked, holding Gwen tight enough to hurt. "Every week?"

"Every day," Gwen promised, though they both knew distance had its own way of changing things.

Her father's Bug sat warming in the driveway, their breath fogging its windows in the cool morning air. The drive to the airport felt like watching her life rewind - past the school with its empty yard, past the pink house where so many lunches had been shared, past fields of sugar cane stretching green and endless toward mountains that had held her whole world until now.

At the airport, her father's hands shook as he checked her bags. "You mudda..." he started, then stopped, swallowed hard. "She would be proud, you know. Of who you becoming."

Security gates waited ahead, marking the point where she'd have to walk forward alone. Sharon's package felt warm in her hands, Lenwell's sugar cane pressed safe in her pocket, her father's tears falling silent on her shoulder as he held her one last time.

"Me go be alright," she whispered, not sure if she was promising him or herself.

His smooth voice caught on the words: "Me know, child. Me know." Then softer, rougher: "Me love you, you hear?"

She walked through security without looking back, knowing if she turned, if she saw her father's eyes or thought about Lenwell standing under their mango tree, she might not find the strength to keep walking.

The plane lifted into morning sky, carrying her toward a future she hadn't chosen but had to live anyway. Below, St. Kitts grew smaller - the mountains, the cane fields, the life she was leaving - until everything blurred together like memory, like tears, like love that had to be enough even when distance tried to prove otherwise.

In her pocket, Lenwell's sugar cane stayed sweet against her fingers. In her heart, everything else she couldn't pack - her mother's smile, her father's smooth voice, Sharon's laughter, Lenwell's kisses - beat steady as waves against the shore of home.

More Books by Leah T. Williams

If you enjoyed this book, check out more stories by Leah T. Williams:

Neither Out Far Nor In Deep – A Caribbean coming-of-age story about finding home in unexpected places. **Also available as an audiobook wherever audiobooks are sold.**

Where Is Noemi – A gripping young adult mystery about a sister's disappearance and the secrets hidden in plain sight.

Where The Guava Tree Stands – A beautifully crafted

novel in verse, weaving family, culture, and the mysteries of the past.

Find my books at all major online retailers, including **Amazon, Barnes & Noble, Apple Books, Kobo, and Walmart**. They are also available on **Hoopla**, so be sure to check your local library!

Support Independent Authors

If you loved this book, **please leave a review!** Your feedback helps more readers discover my stories and supports my journey as an independent author. Even a few words make a big difference!

Connect With Me

Follow me on social media: **@kittiwriter1**
Visit my website: **www.leahtwilliams.net**

Thank you for reading and supporting my work!